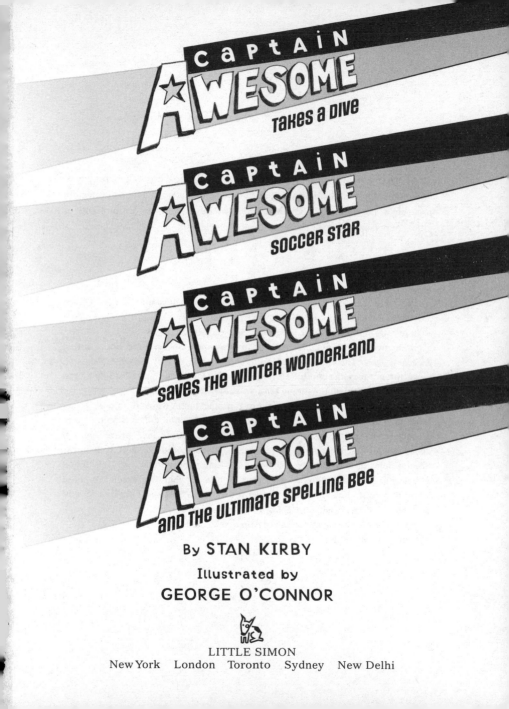

Captain AWESOME TAKES A DIVE

Captain AWESOME SOCCER STAR

Captain AWESOME SAVES THE WINTER WONDERLAND

Captain AWESOME AND THE ULTIMATE SPELLING BEE

By STAN KIRBY

Illustrated by
GEORGE O'CONNOR

LITTLE SIMON
New York   London   Toronto   Sydney   New Delhi

LITTLE SIMON

An imprint of Simon & Schuster Children's Publishing Division

New York   London   Toronto   Sydney   New Delhi

1230 Avenue of the Americas, New York, New York 10020

Captain Awesome Takes a Dive; *Captain Awesome, Soccer Star*; and *Captain Awesome Saves the Winter Wonderland* copyright © 2012 by Simon & Schuster, Inc. *Captain Awesome and the Ultimate Spelling Bee* copyright © 2013 by Simon & Schuster, Inc. This Little Simon bind-up edition 2015.

Manufactured in the United States of America 0615 FFG 10 9 8 7 6 5 4 3 2

ISBN 978-1-4814-5091-1

Contents

Table of Contents

Could time go any s-l-o-w-e-r? When would summer vacation ever get here!?

Eugene McGillicudy sat at his desk in Ms. Beasley's class. His Super Dude Digital Command Watch counted down the remaining minutes.

What's that?!

You've never heard of Super Dude, the greatest, most powerful superhero on several planets?

The superhero who once defeated Mower Mouth, the big, mean-mouth Martian that devoured yards and soccer fields with its Mower Martian Mouth?

Without Super Dude's comic books, Eugene would never have become Captain Awesome or formed the Sunnyview Superhero Squad with his best friend, Charlie Thomas Jones, also known as . . . Nacho Cheese Man!

Only six more minutes—three hundred sixty seconds!—stood between Eugene and Charlie's seventy-one super summer days of fighting evil in Sunnyview. Not once would he have to hear things like his teacher saying, "Please take your seats."

Eugene had even made a list of his summer plans:

1. Learn to be the best swimmer ever.

2. Sleep as late as possible.

3. Stop evil from eviling.

DING-DING-ABING-BING!

THAT WAS THE BELL!

FINALLY!

SUMMER! VACATION! HAD! OFFICIALLY! BEGUN!

Eugene rocketed to his cubby. "Let's go, Charlie!"

Aside from putting evil on an asteroid prison orbiting the twin moons of See Ya Later, is there anything better than summer vacation? Eugene sure didn't think so.

Charlie packed up his cheese

containers from his cubby and stuffed them in his backpack. Nacho Cheese Man's Dairy Defense couldn't be left at school for the entire summer. There's no telling what bad guys would do if they got their evil hands on the cheesy goodness of Hot Jalapeño Surprise or Titanic Taco Blast.

Plus the expiration dates were in July.

"See ya later, My! Me! Mine! Mere-DITH!" Eugene said and waved to Meredith Mooney.

Meredith stuck up her nose and stomped out of the class.

"No school, no homework, and no Meredith for a whole summer!" Charlie cheered. "I don't know which one I'll miss the *least*."

Eugene picked up Turbo's ball. After all, superheroes can't go on patrol without their trusty hamster sidekicks. All three left the classroom.

It was time for one last school patrol!

Eugene and Charlie headed down the hall. Lockers were open, papers were scattered everywhere. It looked like Messypotamian, the slobby villain who never cleaned his room, had returned to mess up the school.

BOOM! **CRASH!** **KLANG!**

"Evil sounds from the cafeteria!" Charlie gasped.

The boys raced to the lunchroom, flung open the doors, and saw true evil.

The two boys dove for cover.

"It's our old enemy, Dr. Yuck Spinach!" Eugene whispered.

"He must've escaped from Asteroid Prison and returned to

continue his evil vegetable plans!"

"There's only one way out of this veggie trap—" Eugene said. "A direct charge through Dr. Spinach's Cafeteria Lair."

"That's insane!" Charlie gasped. "We will never make it! He'll use his Okra Bombs and Asparagus Spears!"

"Yes. And his Parsnips of Doom, too," Eugene replied. "But Super Dude never says never!"

It's time for action!

"CHAAAAARGE!" he shouted and raced into the cafeteria!

BOUNCE!

Oops!

Eugene tripped over the doorway and flopped to the floor.

ROLL!

Turbo's plastic ball flew from Eugene's hands and rolled across the cafeteria floor . . . stopping at Dr. Spinach's feet.

"EEEPS!" Charlie gasped in horror as Dr. Spinach turned to pick up Turbo.

"What have we here?" the evil chef of leafy green yuckiness growled.

Eugene and Charlie yanked their costumes from their back-packs.

"Don't touch my sidekick!" Captain Awesome yelled in his evil-fighting voice.

"You shall not harm Turbo on this day, Dr. Yuck Spinach! Not if Captain Awesome and I, Nacho Cheese Man, have anything to say about it!" Nacho Cheese Man shouted in his evil-fighting voice as well. Then, the superhero friends leaped into action.

CHAPTER 2

Danger Is a
Wet and Stinky
Diaper Queen

By Eugene

"Marco!" Eugene closed his eyes and called out across the pool, looking for Charlie.

"Polo!" Charlie called back. He floated like the Super Silent Crocodilios from Super Dude's Holiday Special No. 2.

It was Saturday, the first day of summer vacation, and Eugene and Charlie were splashing and swimming at the Sunnyview Community Center swimming pool. The sun was high in the sky and that made the water feel like a bath without soap.

The boys had been playing Marco Polo for only a few minutes when Charlie felt inspired. "Let's play Super Dude Polo!"

The rules of Super Dude Polo were from the Super Dude Summer Vacation Special No. 3. That comic was so rare, the only known copy was in the Super Dude Museum in

Blacksburg, Virginia. Fortunately, the rules were posted online!

Charlie had them memorized:

"The rules of Super Dude Polo are very simple. Player one closes his eyes and calls out the first half of a Super Dude villain's name. Player two, whose eyes are not closed, responds by saying the second half of the name, then tries to get away before player one can find him."

Eugene eagerly agreed and closed his eyes.

"Sir Stinky . . . !" Eugene called out.

"Stinkopotomus!" Charlie called back.

Eugene dove for the sound of Charlie's voice, but Charlie swam away laughing.

"Commander Barf . . . !" Eugene yelled.

"Pudding!!" Charlie replied,

clapping his hands.

Eugene jumped to the right, but Charlie wasn't there.

"Mr. Mad . . . !" Eugene called out once more.

"Haturday!"

Eugene was locked on to Charlie this time, but before Eugene could grab him, something brushed against his back.

BRUSH!

Was that Charlie horsing around, or was it something worse?

Eugene opened his eyes. It was worse.

Their most worstest enemy, Queen Stinkypants from the Planet Baby, bobbed up and down in her evil Giraffe Floatie! She unleashed the kicking power of her terrible Surprise Splash Attack!

"Look out!" Eugene pushed Charlie out of the way of incoming danger.

The water splashed in Eugene's face. "My eyes!" he yelped. "I'm soaked with watery evil!"

While Eugene rubbed the evil from his eyes, Charlie leaped into action.

"I'll put an end to this!" Charlie reached for a can of his powerful squirt cheese—but where was it?

Then he remembered! He'd left his cans on the side of the pool.

OOPS!

"Grble-drble! Grble-drble-drble!"
Queen Stinkypants cackled and then
unleashed the annoying power of her
Baby Laugh. Eugene and Charlie
covered each other's ears, then realized that wouldn't work and covered
their own.

The Queen's Baby Laugh was
much more than just annoying. It
was a call that unleashed her wild

pack of hungry superhero-eating Electric Piranha Sharks!

CHOMP!

"Time to give those sharks a superhero meal with a side order of butt-kicking!" Captain Awesome announced.

He and Nacho Cheese Man took a deep breath and started to swim toward the chomping electric fish . . . .

CHAPTER 3

Don't Trust a Dude with a Whistle

By
Eugene

BREET-TWEET-TWEET!

Eugene heard the whistle first. Was it an alarm? A secret signal? Was Queen Chlorina about to turn everyone's eyes red and make their skin itch?

"Hey, little dudes!"

Eugene looked up. It wasn't Queen Chlorina after all. It was Ted, the teenage lifeguard. His long blond hair reflected the sun like

aluminum foil. He wore a green Westville Swim Team tank top.

"There's no running around my pool." Lifeguard Ted pointed out the dangers of running: slipping, sliding, falling, bumping your head, breaking an arm or leg, chipping a tooth, stubbing a toe, falling into the pool, . . . and a whole lot more.

"And can you dudes be careful in the shallow end 'cause there are even littler dudes in the little dude part."

Clearly Ted had no idea about the evils of Scuba-Doobot. *If he*

knew the truth about what was at the bottom of the pool, he'd be running too, thought Eugene.

"Eugene!" Eugene's mother called him from the pool steps. The danger had not passed, for Eugene now faced the most awesome enemy of all time: Getting in Trouble with Mom!

"I thought I told you boys to behave at the pool!" Eugene's mom said. "Horsing around like that is dangerous!"

Eugene knew what that meant: no Super Dude Ice Poptacular to eat on the way home.

In a matter of minutes, the two dripping wet boys were semidry and sitting in the backseat of the car. It was a long, silent ride home. But it gave Eugene plenty of time to think.

That explains that lifeguard's Westville Swim Team tank top.

Lifeguard Ted must really be **the Double-Dipper**, a secret, spying double agent. That's just like a guy from Westville, thought Eugene.

That was when Eugene heard the blast of the Giant Whistle of Doom.

BREET-TWEET-TWEET!

Eugene and Charlie looked out the window. It was the sneaky Double-Dipper himself—half boy, half grown-up, all bad!

The Double-Dipper's greatest and sneakiest superpower was getting superheroes in trouble using his Tattletale Attack!

"You tattletaled on the wrong good guys, villain . . . ," Eugene said quietly.

"**C**hocolate chip cookies are the greatest thing since Super Dude No. 243!" Eugene said. His mouth was so stuffed, it really sounded like: "Chclt ch coos arf fee glate thin imf supf duf two fotty."

Charlie understood every word and said "Yeah!," but it sounded like "Ehhh" because his mouth was full of chocolate chip cookies too.

Eugene swallowed. "Your mom makes the best Cosmic Chip

Cookies in the universe!"

"Only the best for the Super-hero Squad's Weekly Sleepover Meeting!" Charlie stated, grabbing another cookie.

Stuffed full of cosmic goodness, Eugene and Charlie plotted out tomorrow's adventure. They were going back to the community pool to start swimming lessons.

"After we learn to dive like fish, evil won't be able to run, fly, or *swim* from the Sunnyview Super-hero Squad!" Eugene said.

Charlie's dad entered the bedroom carrying the Turbomobile with him. "Hi, boys. I mean, excuse the intrusion, heroes of Sunnyview," he said. Turbo was pressed against the plastic ball, squeaking at Charlie and Eugene. "Turbo rolled all the way to the TV room."

"Sorry, Dad," Charlie said.

"He might've heard some evil outside."

"No problem. Your mom wanted me to remind you that you left your swimsuits outside."

SWIMSUITS!

"Only one more day until swimming lessons begin!" Charlie shouted.

"MI-TEE!" Eugene shouted so loudly that Mr. Jones decided it was time to return to the TV room. He was getting used to hearing "MI-TEE!" around the house whenever Eugene was around.

Once Mr. Jones was gone, Eugene thought he heard a growl. Maybe Charlie's dad was playing a trick on them?

GRRR!

There it was again! Eugene knew that was no playful Dad-growl—it was the horrible, slobbery growl of—

"Mr. Drools!" Eugene shouted.

"He's back!" cried Charlie.

The swimsuits! Eugene thought immediately. *My Captain Awesome Swimming Battlesuit is hanging outside with Nacho Cheese Man's Cheddartrunks!*

Sometimes superheroes protected whole towns. Other times they protected people, but sometimes superheroes needed to protect their Swimming Battlesuits from the terrible slobber of Mr. Drools. No evil dog from the Howling Paw Nebula would ruin their swimming lessons!

CHAPTER 5

Everybody into the Pool!

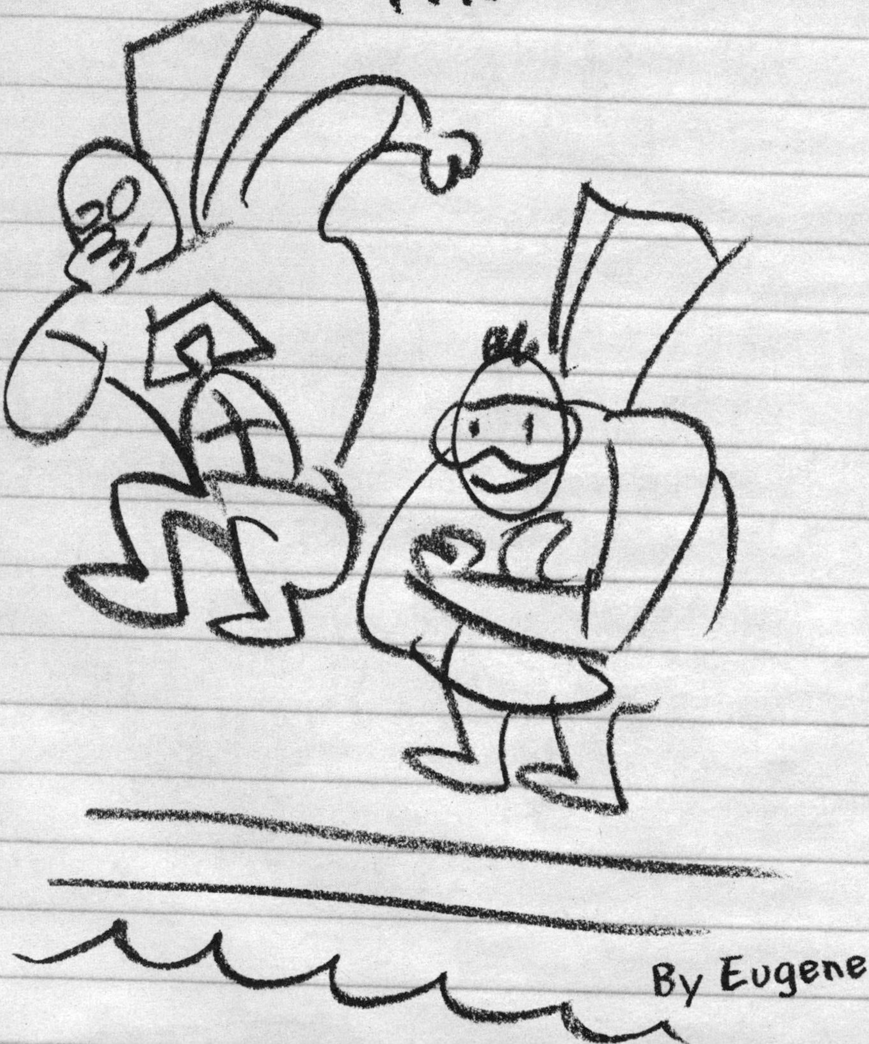

By Eugene

"**W**hy look, it's Puke-Gene and his friend Barfy Jones."

UGH.

Eugene knew that voice could only belong to one person on the planet: Meredith Mooney.

So much for our Meredith-free summer, thought Eugene.

"Hello, My! Me! Mine! Mere-DITH!!" Eugene said, rolling his eyes.

Being Meredith, she was of course wearing a bright pink swimsuit and matching pink goggles.

"She probably has barfy pink flippers and a matching barfy pink kickboard in her mom's car," Charlie whispered to Eugene.

It was the first day of swimming lessons and Meredith wasn't

the only person from Eugene and Charlie's class who was learning to swim.

Sally Williams was there, too. And Bernie Melnik and Evan Mason. It was like a regular school day, except instead of homework there was water. And no desks because . . . they'd sink.

BREET-TWEET-TWEET!

Eugene knew that sound! It was the whistle of his old enemy Ted the Lifeguard, back to tattle a tale once more and make sure another kid wouldn't get his Super Dude Ice Poptacular!

"What ho, little dudes," he said. "Welcome to my swim class."

SHOCK!

GASP!

SHOCK AGAIN!

The Double-Dipper is our swim teacher?

Charlie nudged Eugene. This was badness without any goodness. "We're really going to have to watch this guy," Charlie whispered.

TWEET!

"Into the pool, swimmer dudes," Ted said.

SPLASH!

Once in the water the class hung on to the side of the pool and started kicking.

"That's the way, dudes,"Ted said. "You're doing awesome." He even had a compliment for Mere-DITH. "Gnarly kick, dudette!"

Gnarly kick? Does the Double-Dipper not know that Meredith Mooney is secretly Little Miss Stinky Pinky, the grossest, pinkest villain in all the school systems in the universe and the galaxy?

The forces of good could never let stinky pink villains do better— even when it came to poolside kicking! On land, superheroes were fantastic, but in the water, they must be *splashtastic*!

Little Miss Stinky Pinky had to be splashed

before her show-offyness took total control of the swim class and turned everyone into stinky pink brain zombies.

PLUS! The Double-Dipper needed to know that Captain Awesome and Nacho Cheese Man were wise to his double agent ways.

Eugene and Charlie counted, "One, two, three . . . MI-TEE!" The boys kicked their feet like they were chasing Mr. Drools. Water splashed everywhere! They kicked faster!

SPLISH!

And faster!

SPLASH!

And faster!

SPLISH! SPLASH! SPLOSH!

Little Miss Stinky Pinky squealed like pink villains do when they get wet, and the Double-Dipper ran for cover. Evil is no match for the splashing might of the Superhero Squad!

"Charlie! Eugene! Out of the pool!" Ted yelled. "Not cool, dudes. Uncool!"

OOPS.

Eugene and Charlie climbed up from the pool.

I guess swimming lessons are over for today, thought Eugene.

"Dudes, why don't you chill with some dudely time-outs," Ted suggested.

Eugene and Charlie headed to the snack bar. They were sure to get double-dipped when Ted tattletaled to their moms that they were mis-behaving at the pool again.

But evil had been stopped and covered in water!

"A Super Dude Ice Poptacular is just what we need!" Eugene said.

"Nothing more poptacular

after a hard day of splashing bad guys," Charlie agreed.

But the man behind the counter had a different idea.

"Why don't you boys have something healthier?" a familiar, evil voice threatened.

"YUCK!" the friends gasped.

That's right! Dr. Yuck Spinach, the evil cackling chef from Sunnyview Elementary cafeteria was

now working at the pool's snack shop!

That's what he was doing after school; he was getting ready to serve his awful vegetable surprises to all the summer swimmers. He was even wearing his hairnet. Looks like evil had a part-time summer job!

But no one wants to eat peas or zucchini in the summer!

On a hot day!

At. The. Pool!

DOUBLE YUCK!

If the evil Dr. Spinach wouldn't serve Super Dude Ice Poptaculars to Eugene and Charlie, maybe he'd hand them over to Captain Awesome and Nacho Cheese Man. . . .

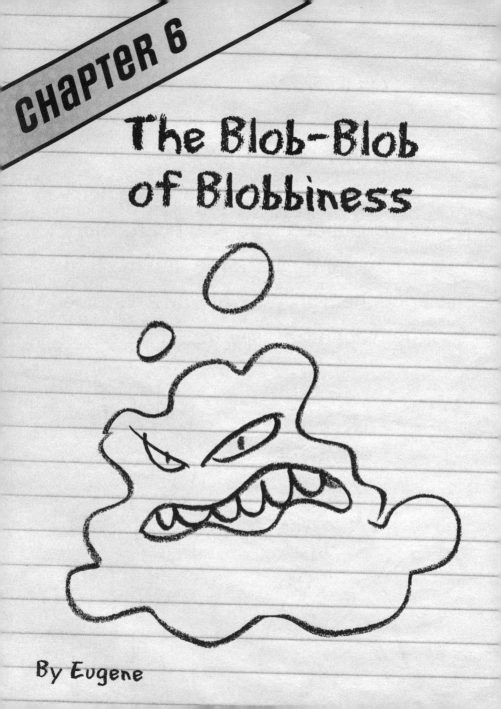

"**O**kay, little swimmers! Give your swim buddy a high five for a job well done!" Ted called out at the end of the next day's lesson. "Class is over, so enjoy some pool time until your parental units arrive."

Eugene gave Charlie a high five. "Not waves nor chlorine nor

public swimming pool pee-pee will keep us from our goal of becoming the best swimmers in the universe. Those were some MI-TEE kicks you did, Charlie."

"You too, Eugene," Charlie replied. "I think we earned some floating time in the shallow end."

Unfortunately, there were only two pool noodles. One was blue and the other was—*GASP!*—PINK and looked like Mr. Drools had been chewing on it.

"*You* take the blue, Charlie. You earned it," Eugene insisted.

"Are you sure, Eugene? We could just sit on the steps."

"No one said being a superhero would be easy," Eugene reminded his best friend. "Sometimes in the battle for goodness you just gotta take the pink noodle floatie."

Eugene jumped back into the pool and lay across his pink floatie. The water was warm, the sun was warmer, and the young superhero

had nothing to do but breathe. There were only two words for a day like that.

"MI-TEE . . ." Eugene sighed.

Actually, it was really only one word, but Eugene was a superhero, able to do super things . . . like make one word sound like two.

"Oh, look at the two little babies, floating in the shallow end like scaredy-babies crying for their mommies!" Meredith's annoying voice shouted from across the pool.

Charlie sat up and looked around. "Who let BABIES in the pool?!"

Eugene didn't answer. He knew very well whom Meredith was calling a baby. The fact that he had chosen the pink noodle floatie didn't help. Eugene expected to see Meredith playing in the water next to them. He looked up and that's when he saw SHE WAS IN THE DEEP END!

"Stay calm. Make no sudden moves," Eugene whispered. "Charlie, this just got serious."

"What's wrong? You afraid there's a big, bad monster in the deep end?" Meredith taunted. "Why don't you two just stay down there and splash with the other babies?"

"We can't let her talk to us like that!" Charlie said.

"Of course not," Eugene said. "She's given me a great idea."

SLAPPP!

Eugene and Charlie slapped their hands in the water as hard as they could.

SPLASH!

A big wave of water rolled across the pool and splashed Meredith.

BULLSEYE!

Her pinkest pink ribbons washed out of her hair. There was nothing Meredith could do now, so she stuck out her tongue.

Eugene felt so good about their splashy victory over Meredith that it didn't seem so bad that he was floating around the pool on the pink noodle that kept sinking.

But then he saw IT!

A . . .

Strange . . .

BLOB!

And it waited silently—as most

blobs do—at the **VERY BOTTOM OF THE DEEP END!** If this were a monster movie, scary music would be blasting! People would be screaming! Panic would spread across the planet!

Eugene didn't move a muscle.

"Stay calm. Make no sudden moves," Eugene whispered. "Charlie, this just got serious."

"Not again!" Charlie gasped.

"This time . . . even more," Eugene whispered.

"EVEN MORE?!" Charlie gasped louder. "Wait. Even more than what?"

"Even more than last time it was serious!" Eugene warned.

"Wow. That *is* serious."

"On the count of three, I want you to panic as loudly as you can and swim like the Jelly Squirrels from Super Dude No. 32," Eugene quietly explained, afraid to take his eyes off the mysterious blob down below.

"One . . . two . . ."

"Panic like a Jelly Squirrel!"

Charlie screamed and, well, pan-
icked exactly like a Jelly Squirrel.

Charlie's panic made Eugene
panic! Eugene's panic made
Charlie panic even more! And
Charlie's even-more panic made
Eugene panic even double-more!

SPLASH! KICK! SWIM!

SLIP! **SINK!**

Sink?! That is *not* a word you want to hear on your second day of swimming lessons! And probably not even on your *third* day, either!

Eugene slipped from his floatie.

His arms slapped at the water. His legs kicked hard, waiting for the Blobby Blob-Blob from the Deep End to grab him by the ankles.

"Hold on little dude!" Ted shouted and raced toward Eugene.

And then, like an ice cream sundae with a cherry on top arriving to save

the day after
a big plate of
boiled carrots, a hand
appeared before Eugene's
face.

"Grab my hand!" the voice shouted.

Eugene didn't need to be told twice. He grabbed the hand and pulled himself safely to the edge of the pool.

"Thanks," Eugene gasped.

"No worries, Eugene," a voice

replied. Eugene froze. It wasn't
Ted's voice. It was a *girl's*.

The pool water cleared from
Eugene's eyes and he realized he
was holding Sally Williams's hand.

Oh man! The only thing worse

than being saved by a girl is holding her hand afterward!

GIRL HAND! BLECH!

Eugene yanked his hand back.

"I guess we're kinda equal now since you found Mr. Whiskersworth for me."

"Yeah. I guess."

Eugene's replies were limited to as few words as possible. His face was redder than the Human Tomato's *Atsa Lotsa Pasta Sauce* that Super Dude always bought from his local grocer.

"Whoa! Are you okay, little

dude?" Ted asked, rushing over to Eugene and Sally.

Eugene nodded.

"Rad save, Sally!" Ted smiled to Sally and gave her a high five.

"Don't worry, Ted. I do this kind of thing all the time." Sally smiled and high-fived him.

Eugene raised an eyebrow and snapped a look to Sally. Eugene wasn't sure if Sally meant that she-saved people all the time or gave high fives.

The thought of Sally as a hero was a strange one, but it wasn't the strangest thing of all. Who sent the evil Blobby Blob-Blob from the Deep End to blob Eugene?

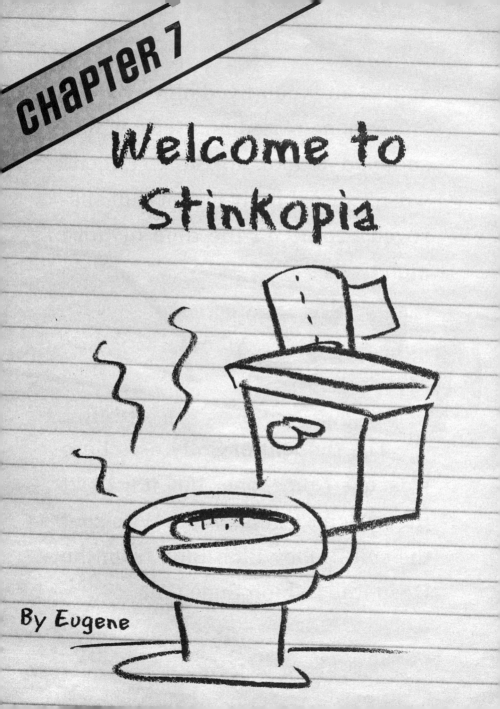

"Okay, little swimmers! Today you little dudes and dudettes get to take turns diving off the side of the pool," Ted announced.

"Isn't it too shallow here?" Meredith asked.

"Confirm-o-mento, Mere," Ted replied. "And that's why we'll be jumping into the pool **in the deep end!**"

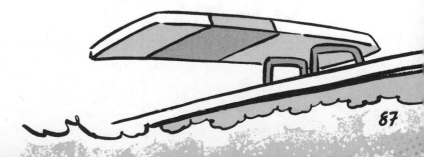

The kids cheered! The kids splashed! The kids high-fived! Well, all the kids but *one* to be exact.

"IN THE DEEP END!"
"IN THE DEEP END!"
"IN THE DEEP END!"

The words echoed over and over

in Eugene's head like a broken parrot robot. The thought of going back to the deep end gave Eugene a funny twisting in his stomach, even worse than the time he snuck some of Charlie's spicy jalapeño cheese.

The other kids in swim class climbed from the pool and walked to the far side. Didn't they know that the Blobby Blob-Blob from the Deep End might still be down there waiting to blob them!?

Eugene climbed from the pool and tugged on Ted's hand.

"What's up, Dude-gene?" Ted asked.

"I . . . um . . . I . . . need to go to the bathroom!"Eugene was already racing away before the last word left his mouth.

Eugene ran into the boy's bathroom and locked himself in one of the bathroom stalls.

It's no big deal, Eugene thought. *I'm sure Super Dude locked himself in a bathroom before.*

Eugene tried to calm himself. He inhaled deeply.

PEE-YEW!

Bad idea! Eugene was in a stinky bathroom!

"Come on, Eugene!" he said to himself. "Instead of hiding here in Stinkopia, you should be out fighting the Blobby Blob-Blob from the Deep End! Who knows what blobby

I.P. FREELY WAS HERE.

blobness that blob will be blobbing on everyone!"

"Stand back, villain, or else prepare to be cheesed by Nacho Cheese Man!" Charlie rushed into the bathroom, dripping wet and blasting cheese. But instead of seeing Eugene trapped by a villainous villain, Charlie was met by an empty bathroom now covered in cheese.

"Aw, man. What a waste of good cheese," Charlie sighed, then added, "You in here Eugene?"

"Over here," Eugene called out from the stall.

"I knew it!" Charlie shouted. "Were you attacked by the Toilet of Terror? Hold on! I'll save you from its Flush of Fear!

"I'm fine," Eugene lied. "It's just . . . I think I ate one too many Super Dude Ice Poptaculars, that's all."

"Oh,"Charlie said, disappointed his friend wasn't stuck in an evil toilet, fighting against the Flush of Fear. "You've been gone for like a jillion minutes. Ted said you're going to miss your turn to dive . . ."

"Um . . . yeah. Can you tell him that's okay? Maybe next time?"

Eugene sat quietly and listened

to Charlie leave. The twisting in his stomach was replaced with a dull ache—one that seemed to wrap itself around his heart.

That *had* to be it, right? One too many Super Dude Ice Poptaculars? After all, superheroes like Super Dude don't get scared.

But, maybe, their secret identities do. . . .

No matter how Eugene twisted, turned, or moved, he couldn't fall asleep. How could he? Tomorrow was Friday.

Isn't Friday the most awesomest of awesome days? Even during summer vacation Friday was like the best parts of Monday, Tuesday, Wednesday, and Thursday all rolled up into one day called Monuesnesursday. It was pizza day at school and THE night for Sunnyview Superhero Squad Sleepovers.

BUT!

This Friday meant something else. It was the last day of Eugene's swim lessons. Eugene would have to jump off the diving board and into . . . *the deep end.*

Eugene couldn't remember the last time he felt this unawesome, but it probably involved his mom and the words "vegetables," "no," and "dessert."

Eugene plopped back onto his bed and covered his face with his pillow.

"Blah!" he groaned.

Turbo raced on his squeaky

wheel, getting his little muscles ready for their next mission. Eugene sat up and stared at his sidekick. Turbo stopped running. He looked right at Eugene and said, "Squeak! Squeak!"

"You're right, Turbo! We have to be brave! That's what superheroes do!" Eugene climbed from his bed. He clenched his fists and puffed out his chest, because heroic moments like this required chest-puffing.

"It's our job to protect the Sunnyview Community Pool from the Blobby Blob-Blob from the Deep End! And no blobby blob-blob is gonna stop me from doing it!"

It was here . . . the last day of swim class!

With a newfound courage in his heart (Eugene had thanked Turbo for the pep talk the night before), Eugene arrived at the pool ready for action.

"Try not to get sick on Super Dude Ice Poptaculars today, Eugenio!" Meredith giggled.

Eugene ignored Meredith. For one, she looked pinker than cotton candy with pigtails, and for two, Eugene was on a mission.

"Okay, C-man!" Ted said to Charlie. "You get to go for the big dive first!"

Charlie gave a quick smile and thumbs-up to Eugene. Everyone was watching Charlie, so Eugene took two slow, silent steps away from the group, then raced toward the locker room.

Charlie stopped at the end of the diving board and looked into the water below. There was something in the pool! Something . . .

BLOBBY!

"Go ahead, C-Man! I've got you covered!" Ted called up to him.

"But there's something in the pool," Charlie replied.

"I'm here for you, Nacho Cheese Man!" Captain Awesome shouted as he rushed to the diving board. Captain Awesome threw a can of cheese and Charlie snagged it in midair.

"What are you *doing*, Eugene?" Charlie whispered once Captain Awesome joined him.

"Saving you from Little Miss Stinky Pinky's Blobby Blob-Blob!"

And with those brave words,

Captain Awesome dove into the water!

"MI-TEEEEEEEEEE!"

"Whoa," a stunned Ted said, then turned to the other kids and asked, "Who's Nacho Cheese Man?"

Under water, Captain Awesome dove to the bottom to battle with the Blobby Blob-Blob from the Deep.

The Blobby Blob-Blob squirmed and wormed, but Captain Awesome would not let it go. He burst to the surface, the dreaded creature firmly clenched in his superhands.

"Not all your blobbiness shall save you from my awesome grip of goodness!" Captain Awesome said as he wrestled the creature.

"Hold on, Captain Awesome!" Charlie called out from above and dove into the water. A can of nacho cheese squirted wildly in his hand.

"Whoa," a stunned Ted said, then turned to the other kids and asked, "Who's Captain Awesome?"

"**T**hanks for the save, Captain Awesome. I don't know what would've happened if I jumped off that diving board without you there to help me." Charlie stuck the can of cheese in his mouth and gave a suck, then offered it to Captain Awesome. "Want some?"

But Captain Awesome had more on his mind than cheese. The Blobby Blob-Blob from the Deep

End lay on the ground, looking less blobby and evil than it had before getting Captain Awesome's 1-2 Underwater Punch.

"Look!" Captain Awesome gasped. "The Blobby Blob-Blob looks like a green giraffe!"

"I always knew giraffes were evil!" Charlie said, hitting his palm with his fist.

But it wasn't just an evil giraffe. It was Eugene's baby sister Molly's deflated giraffe floatie! It had popped and sunk to the bottom of the pool!

"Gah! Goo! Garggelsnansjboo!"

"By all that's gibberish!" cried Captain Awesome at hearing the babbling of his most arch-of-enemies. "Could it be true?! Queen Stinkypants from the Planet Baby teamed up with Little Miss Stinky Pinky?!"

It *was* true! For there sat Queen Stinkypants in a lounge chair right next to Eugene's mom! She was smelly! She was stinky! She was sticky!

Sticky?!

"ARRRRRRRRRR! She's eating my Super Dude Ice Poptacular!" Captain Awesome groaned. "Her terrible trick worked! Why didn't we see her stinky stink was the real evil behind this plot?"

"Because you can't smell evil underwater, C.A. Even stinky evil," Charlie reminded him.

The Super Dude Ice Poptacular may have been lost, but Little Miss Stinky Pinky and Queen Stinkypants were defeated! Captain Awesome's awesome work was done. The Blobby Blob-Blob was defeated and would blobby blob-blob little swimmers no more!

"That was one cool-a-mundo dive, dude," Ted said to Captain Awesome. "But next time, no super-hero costumes allowed in the pool. It's not safe to swim in a cape."

Eugene nodded because super-heroes had to follow the rules.

"I return the pool to your watchful eye, Ted," Captain Awesome said. "Continue your fight against sunburn, swimming too soon after you eat, and running by the pool!"

"Will do, little dude, and don't worry, 'Badness always loses.'"

Did Ted *really* just say Super

Dude's favorite saying?! Ted gave a wink and Captain Awesome knew he was leaving the pool in safe hands. Perhaps Ted was not the tattletale double-agent spy, the Double-Dipper, after all! No fan of Super Dude could ever be anything but awesome.

Captain Awesome smiled before

racing back to the locker room.

"That was one cool little super-dude," Ted said.

★ ★ ★ ★ ★

The day was done, but even more importantly,

swim class was done. Everyone got Ted's "Excellent Swimmer" medals because they were all excellent little swimmers. Eugene took home the best prize of all: Swim Teacher Ted's Best of All High Dive Award.

Eugene's awesome dive as Captain Awesome had earned him

the top honor in his class! That was way better than Meredith's Safest Swimmer Award or Charlie's Most Improved Paddler.

Eugene and Charlie offered a quick wave good-bye. There was no need for anything more, for they'd soon be seeing each other again at the Superhero Squad Sleepover.

It was Friday, after all.

Eugene slid into the backseat of his mom's car. With a quick click of the seat belt, he was safe, secure, and ready to go home. Molly was already in her car seat,

gnawing away at some poor doll's head.

Eugene felt happy. He sat back and closed his eyes. Bad guys, beware! Captain Awesome and

Nacho Cheese Man had once again made Sunnyview safe! No villain was too bad! No pool was too deep! No Blobby Blob-Blob was too blobby!

Only one thing could make this day even more perfect . . .

Eugene's mom closed her door, then reached between the seats and handed something to her son.

"I got you another Super Dude Ice Poptacular since Molly ate yours . . ."

Eugene took the sugary treat and smiled.

MI-TEE!

123

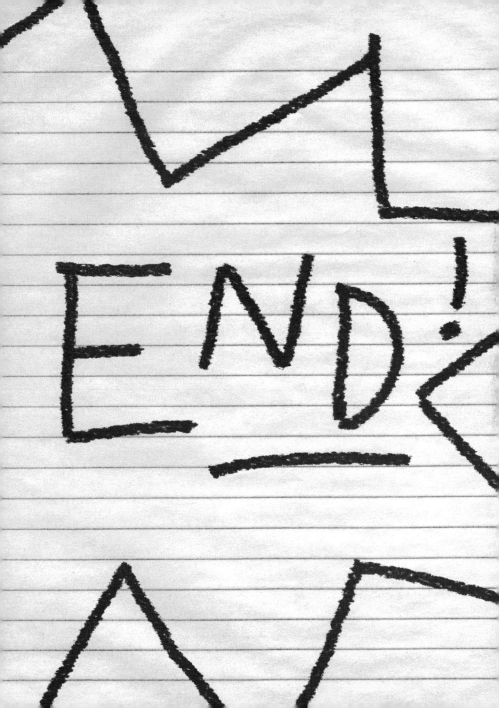

Captain AWESOME,
SOCCER STAR

By STAN KIRBY

Illustrated by
GEORGE O'CONNOR

Table of Contents

FALL!

Is there a worse name for a season than "fall"? Eugene McGillicudy thought as he walked home from Sunnyview Elementary School where he had just escaped from second grade.

Fall. Who names a season after an accident? Are there other seasons called "trip" or "crash" or "oops"?

NO.

So why name it "fall"? Is it really *because* *the* *leaves* *are* *turning* color *and* falling off *the* *trees* *and* *that* *snow* *might* *soon* *be* falling *from* *the* *sky?*

Really? Whatever the reason, it is certainly better than "autumn."

I'd bet no one even knows what that word means, Eugene thought.

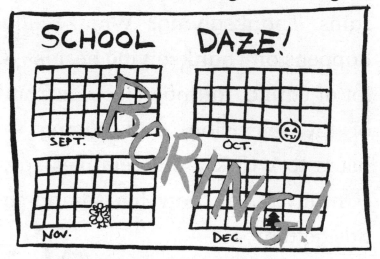

Fall was the most boring, BORING, BO-RING time of year between the start of the school year and winter break—a time when NOTHING happens.

Oh sure, you can say that

there's Halloween, but that's really only for one day and sometimes it rains. Thanksgiving? What *really* happens on Thanksgiving besides a lot of eating, falling asleep in front of the television, and having to listen to wrinkly old relatives say, "Oh, my! Look how big so-and-so has gotten!"

So yeah, there's nothing.

KA-THUNKK!

"OUCH!" cried Eugene, his thoughts now focused on

things hitting his
head.

I'm under attack!
Eugene thought and dove
for cover behind a tree.
But who could it be?!
KA-THUNKK!

"Ouch!" Something
bounced off of his
head again.

"Curse you,
Captain Ka-Thunk!
I know it's you!" Eugene
quickly poked his head out
from behind the tree and

shouted. "You'll not ka-thunk the number one fan of Super Dude without a fight!"

What's that?

You've never heard of Super Dude?

Do you live in a crater on the moon? Actually, if you've never heard of Super Dude, then you'd have to live in a crater on the *dark side* of the moon.

Super Dude is only the greatest superhero ever. He is the star of mountains and *mountains* of comic books, all of which Eugene owned.

Following Super Dude's example, Eugene created his own outfit and became . . .

CAPTAIN AWESOME!

Along with his best friend, Charlie Thomas Jones (also known as the superhero Nacho Cheese Man), and sidekick, Turbo the Hamster, Eugene formed the Sunnyview Superhero Squad to stop evil from eviling in the town of Sunnyview. Sunnyview had a surprising amount of eviling going on.

KA-THUNKK!

Again.

OUCH!

ACORNS!

If it wasn't Captain Ka-Thunk or his Thunkulicious Thunkers, it could only mean one thing!

High in the tree, General Squirrel Nuthatch was chittering away in his rodent language while staring angrily at Eugene. He held another Atomic Acorn in his paws.

"So, General Nuthatch, it seems you have escaped from the Nut House for evil rodents!" Eugene called up. "But it was, dare I say, *nuts* of you to return to Sunnyview to unleash your attack! You and your Atomic Acorns will be a threat to the good people of Sunnyview no longer, for you have ka-thunked the number one Squirrel Stopper in the universe!

"You've gotten a little too squirrely for your own good,

Nuthatch! There's gonna be more than leaves falling off trees this autumn!" Captain Awesome cried out in his most awesome superhero voice.

"MI-TEE!" Captain Awesome shouted as he leaped his bravest leap. . . .

KA-THUNKK!

"OUCH!" cried Eugene as something round hit him in the back of the head. Was he under attack? Again?!

Eugene looked around. What he saw was better. Much better.

It was a soccer ball, and it signaled the start of one of the

classic four seasons of boyhood. Eugene knew the list by heart:

1. Christmas vacation
2. Spring break
3. Summer vacation
4. Soccer season!

"Sorry, Eugene!" It was Charlie, aka Nacho Cheese Man, the second-greatest fighter of evil in Sunnyview. "I was trying to 'bend it' like Sim Simonson, the Arctic Sharks striker, but it was more like my foot 'flopped it.'"

"Like Phillip?" asked Eugene. He pointed across the school yard where Phillip Dickenson tried to kick a soccer ball. He completely missed and flopped on to his back.

"Exactly!" Charlie said. As Phillip rolled over slowly like a roly-poly bug, Charlie pulled a flyer from his pocket. "Check *this* out."

Eugene's Awesome Vision scanned the piece of paper. It was a sign-up sheet for the Sunnyview

SUNNYVIEW
YOUTH SOCCER LEAGUE

EIGHT-YEAR-OLD DIVISION

Youth Soccer League's eight-year-old division.

"We're in!" Eugene said. "Let's sign up!"

The more Eugene thought about it, the more excited he got. By the time he got home for dinner, he was ready to pop like Colonel

Kernel, the human popcorn ball who was defeated by Super Dude in Super Dude No. 14, *Super Dude's Microwave Adventures.*

"Let this be a lesson to you, Colonel Kernel," Super Dude had said, as he tossed the puffy villain in a prison tub. "You'll never be able to defeat the rays of goodness!"

Eugene ran into the living room. "Mom! Dad! Big news! Like, it's bigger than the biggest big thing you can think of!"

Eugene closed the front door. "You're looking at the *almost*

newest member of the Sunnyview
Youth Soccer League!"

"That's a fantastic idea, son,"
Eugene's dad, Ned, said. "Will Charlie
be joining you?"

"Dad! Of course!" Eugene said.
"I'd never join a team without my
best friend."

With *two* superheroes on

Sunnyview's team, they would be unstoppable. *How long would it take to score a million goals ... every game? The soccer games would last for days! Or weeks, even!*

Eugene imagined the sounds of loud cheering.

FINALLY!

Saturday! The big, big day! The soccer team's first practice!

BEEP! BEEP!

"Dad!" Eugene gasped. "Wait!" His dad was already in the car, eager to go. "I'm coming!"

Eugene flew down the stairs, tripped over his feet, bounced off the handrail, boomed off the wall, and caught himself by jumping off

the third stair and landing on the floor below.

"MI-TEE!" Eugene yelled in his most awesome Captain Awesome voice and pointed at the stairs. "Yes! Stairs of Evil, beware! Captain Awesome shall not be tripped by you on Soccer Day!"

Once in the car, it was just a quick drive down the street to pick up Charlie, who eagerly waited on the sidewalk.

"MI-TEE!" Eugene yelled out the car window.

"Cheesy-yo!" Charlie responded, and hopped in.

"We must be on constant watch for evil," Eugene said. He scanned the passing houses as the car turned the corner. "Evil could be

lurking around any corner, behind any trash can, or inside any building or store. It could be anywhere!"

"Except for Ice Cream Coney's," Charlie reminded Eugene. "There's nothing in there but ice cream and toppings. And those are never, ever evil. Only yummy."

"Yummy," both boys said in unison.

"I know what you guys need to do!" Mr. McGillicudy blurted out.

Eugene sank a little lower in his seat, filled with the mixture of dread and embarrassment that only a parent could create. His dad was about to . . .

"Sing!" Eugene's dad continued.

"Sing a song?" Charlie asked, scrunching his nose at the thought.

"Exactly!" Ned said. "A song

will pump you guys up for your first soccer practice!"

Mr. McGillicudy turned on the car's CD player. The car filled with the hideous sounds of HORRIBLE baby music.

"I love this song!" Ned shouted and tapped his fingertips on the steering wheel.

But the stuff coming out of the car speakers was, of course, not really music, but his little sister's favorite song:

the one and only "Monday."

Eugene and Charlie were hit by every evil word.

"I like Monday, Monday, Monday.

"It's the best day, best day, best day.

"I'm so happy, happy, happy!

"It's a Monday, Monday, Monday!"

ARGH!

Eugene and Charlie slapped their hands over their ears!

"Must . . . block out . . . brain-frying . . . sounds!" Eugene groaned.

"Monday, Monday, Monday!"

"Stupid . . . orange Dinosaur Delmer! Gross baby songs . . . crawling into . . . my ears . . . Head will explode like gooey . . . goo!"

Charlie struggled to get the words

out before his head exploded like gooey goo.

"I'm so happy, happy, happy!"

"Queen Stinkypants!" Eugene gasped, referring to the secret evil identity of his baby sister, Molly. "She must've . . . planned this . . . to melt . . . our brains!"

"So we can't . . . play . . . soccer!" Charlie continued.

"Goodness and soccer shall never be . . . defeated by dino

badness and baby songs," Eugene replied. "Only one thing . . . to . . . do . . ."

"SUPER SONIC SCREAM!"

both boys shouted at the same time.

"AAAAAAAAAAAAAA
AAAAAAAAAAAAAAA
AAAAAAAAAAAAA
AAAAH!"

Eugene's dad turned off the CD player. "Boys! What's wrong?!" he asked urgently.

Eugene and Charlie removed their hands, relieved that the ear-melting sounds of the "Happiest Orange Dinosaur in the Happyzoic Era" had been shattered by their Super Sonic Scream.

"It's okay now, Dad." Eugene sighed. "But you have no idea how close you came to having to clean our exploded brains off the ceiling of your car."

"Exploded and *gooey* brains!" Charlie added.

Eugene's dad wasn't entirely sure what the two boys were talking about, but he had just vacuumed the car last Saturday, so he was more than happy to avoid any messes in the backseat.

Especially gooey exploded-brain messes. Mr. McGillicudy thought he would really need to scrub to get that stuff out.

"**G**o!"

Charlie and Eugene zoomed from the car the moment Eugene's dad turned off the engine at Sunnyview Park.

"Boys! Wait for—" But before Eugene's dad could finish his sentence, he was alone in the car. "—me."

"Over there!" Eugene cried, seeing some friends from Sunnyview Elementary. Evan

Mason, Mike Flinch, and Bernie Melnick were already kicking soccer balls and knee juggling.

Eugene charged to the nearest ball. With the explosive shout of "MI-TEE!" he kicked it as hard as he could. The ball zoomed over the grass and came to a stop next to the largest, pinkest blob of cotton candy Eugene had ever seen.

And then the blob moved! It kicked the ball!

Wait a second . . . , Eugene thought as the Annoying Little Girl Siren in his head grew louder. *That's no cotton-candy blob! Arrrgh! It's . . .*

"Well, if it isn't Stinkgene and Charleach!" Meredith Mooney yelled out. She was dressed from head-to-toe in pink, as usual, and smelled like a strawberry bathroom air freshener. "Here to impress us all with your soccer skills?"

"Shouldn't you be looking for the all-girls' cootie team, Meredith?" Eugene teased, wondering where Meredith managed to buy pink soccer shoes.

"Ha! Shows what you know, Eugerm," Meredith replied. "This is *coed* soccer. That means it's for boys *and* girls. You're on *my* team." Meredith laughed the kind of laugh that made the hair on the back of Eugene's neck stand up like the bristles of a toothbrush.

Eugene started to laugh too.

But then he realized no one else was laughing. In fact, Charlie was biting his lower lip and had a  look on his face that made Eugene think he had to go to the bathroom, bad. Like really, *really* bad.

But Charlie didn't need a bathroom break. He needed a Meredith break.

"Girls?!" Charlie gasped when Marlo Craven and Sally Williams joined Meredith. "No one said there'd be girls on the team!"

"This is just a cootie festival disguised as a soccer practice," Eugene said, equally stunned. There was one person who could clear this up right away. "Where's our coach? Does he know there are girls on our team?"

BREET-TWEET-TWEET!

"Surprise!" said Eugene's dad. He ran onto the soccer field wearing a whistle and carrying a big net full of soccer balls.

SHOCK AND HORROR!

"DAD?! *You're* the coach?! Wait. Did you know there were girls on the team?!" Eugene asked.

"Yeah! A coed team! Isn't it great?" Coach McGillicudy replied and dropped the soccer balls on the grass.

But this was not the worst thing that could happen. That would be a rocket ship from Dinosaurus X9 that brought the evil Super Pteranodonald to crush cars and eat Sunnyview.

Although, compared to the thought of playing soccer with Meredith, the pink cotton-candy blob, a superalien dinosaur attack didn't seem like such a bad thing after all.

"We have a lot of practicing to do," Coach McGillicudy said. "Our first big game is next week against the Westville Kickers."

"They're the best team in the league!" Mike Flinch whispered to the others.

"Yeah! I hear they've never been beaten. By anyone. EVER," Sally added.

"Now, before we get started," Coach McGillicudy started. "I've got a little surprise that I think will get everyone pumped up."

PUMPED UP?

Dread and embarrassment Part Two!

Not another orange dinosaur song! Eugene dove on the bag of soccer balls, looking for his dad's MP3 player, so he could rip out the battery pack and hide it forever.

Coach McGillicudy continued as if Eugene's behavior was the most normal thing in the world. And for Eugene, it was.

"I've got uniforms!" Coach McGillicudy proudly announced.

SUNNYVIEW
MEGABYTES

Coach McGillicudy opened a big box and pulled out a stack of bright red shirts. Team jerseys! Names and numbers were on the back. On the front was the team's name: Sunnyview Megabytes.

"Nice, huh?" Coach McGillicudy said. "The Sunnyview Megabytes! I thought of it myself!"

"What's a megabyte?" Charlie asked Eugene. "Is it evil? I can't play on an evil soccer team."

"Don't worry," Eugene replied. "It's some computer word my dad likes to say. A lot."

After they put on their new shirts, Coach McGillicudy ran the team through some soccer drills.

First was dribbling the ball. Eugene tripped over his ball and fell to the ground.

Then there was kicking the ball. Eugene tripped over his ball and fell to the ground.

And finally there was blocking the ball. The ball smacked Eugene in the chest.

And then Eugene tripped over the ball and fell to the ground.

"Okay! Let's start with some passing exercises!" Coach McGillicudy announced. "Everyone split into groups of two!"

Meredith's hand shot up quickly. "I'll pass with Charlie," she declared.

Charlie stiffened and his face scrunched up like he had to go to the bathroom again. He followed Meredith away from the group and looked back briefly to mouth the words *HELP ME!* to Eugene.

Meredith—who was secretly Captain Awesome and Nacho Cheese Man's archrival, Little Miss Stinky Pinky—was obviously up to no good. She was trying to keep the Sunnyview Superhero Squad separated so they wouldn't score their million goals!

Typical villain, thought Eugene. But enough is enough! Little Miss Stinky Pinky did not reckon with the soccer-powered goodness of Captain Awesome. He would never let Nacho Cheese Man be led to his

soccer-kicking defeat.

"Game on!" Captain Awesome shouted as he set to work to save Nacho Cheese Man! "Neither Stinky Pinky, nor cotton-candy blobs, nor the threat of grass stains shall stop me from scoring this goooooaaaaal for goodness!"

SIGH.

The ride home seemed much longer than the ride to the park. Like a billion, jillion years longer. Eugene's excitement was gone, replaced by a dull disappointment in his big soccer debut. How could he score his million goals if the ball kept sneaking under his feet and tripping him?

"If only I was wearing my cape." Eugene sighed

to himself. He always thought better thoughts in a cape.

The CAPE!

That's when it hit him.

The idea.

THE BIGGEST, MOST BIGGER IDEA.

THE AWESOMEST, MOST AWESOME IDEA, EVER!

Yes, Eugene would absolutely

wear his Captain Awesome outfit for the first big Megabytes game next Saturday! There would be no stopping him if he played as Captain Awesome. He'd kick supergoals with his left foot and then superer goals with his right foot and then supererest goals with his left and right foot at the same time!

VICTORY!

The rest of the week was a blur of school, lunch, homework, and looking for evil. It seemed like forever for those seven days to pass, but by the next Saturday, Eugene was ready and, more importantly, so was his Captain Awesome outfit.

Eugene secretly packed it into his backpack and grabbed the Turbomobile, the clear plastic ball Captain Awesome's hamster sidekick, Turbo, used to patrol for evil.

Warm-up drills got off to a great start! Eugene only tripped over the ball twice. The ball only hit him in the head once. And that was a stray ball from the other team.

Eugene kicked it back to the Kickers and took a short break with Charlie to check them out.

"They've got matching pants," Charlie said.

"Just like the Doom Legion of

Smartypants in Super Dude No. 64," Eugene said. "We can beat these guys."

"Okay, team! Gather round!" Coach McGillicudy called out. "We've got five minutes before the game against the Kickers starts, so listen up!"

Charlie and the other members of the Sunnyview Megabytes jogged over to their coach. Everyone except for Eugene, that is.

In a flash Eugene snuck from the group, raced behind the snack shed, and unzipped his backpack! Inside lay his only hope, folded rather nicely and smelling of springtime fabric softener: his Captain Awesome outfit!

BREET-TWEET-TWEET!

The referee's whistle! The game was starting!

Captain Awesome zoomed from behind the snack shed and ran onto the soccer field with the most heroic run in the history of heroic running.

"Never fear, Megabytes!" Captain Awesome said. "Captain Awesome is here to lead our team to victory and score a million goals! **MI-TEE!**"

But instead of being greeted with the adoring cheers of the crowd, Captain Awesome only heard the shrill sound of **_BREET-TWEET-TWEET!_**

The referee held up a yellow card. "Yellow card!" he cried out,

calling the
penalty   against
Eugene. "Entering the field of play
without permission. Also wearing a
cape. No capes allowed."

Coach McGillicudy had to pull
Eugene from the field.

"But . . . but . . . I *need* my
cape!" a stunned Captain Awesome

explained. "I'm Captain Awesome!"

"I don't care if you're Santa Claus," the referee replied. "It's the rules."

Eugene looked at his dad, his friends, and finally back to the referee. And then it dawned on him. This was no ordinary soccer official. The striped shirt, the loud whistle, and the cards of yellow and red should have been clues.

If only I hadn't been so concerned about

scoring a million goals, I would've noticed sooner!

Captain Awesome thought. Mental note: Next time only worry about scoring a half-million goals, so I can focus more on the very evil standing right in front of my face!

This "referee" was really the evil **Whistleblower**, the superannoying supervillain with his Noisy Whistle of Annoyance and Ouch-That-Hurts-My-Ears-Ness.

"Blow all you want with your mighty evil lungs, Whistleblower!"

Captain Awesome said to the villain. "Nothing shall stop Captain Awesome from scoring the winning goal for all that's good and true!"

There's really no reason to ask who the best player was on the Sunnyview Megabytes.

"ME!" Meredith would shout before you even finished the question. And the sad thing? She was right.

Not only was Meredith the best player on the team, she was also the pinkest girl in all of Sunnyview, certainly the world, and maybe even the whole universe, including the craters of the moon.

Eugene returned after removing his Captain Awesome outfit. Wearing his regular team jersey, he joined the two teams on the field, and the Westfield Kickers captain kicked off. Meredith controlled the ball and worked it downfield, dashing and darting between the Westfield Kickers players.

"I'm open! Pass the ball!" Eugene called out.

Meredith passed the ball to

Charlie, who sent it to Marlo. She boinged it off her forehead, sending it back to Charlie who passed it to Meredith.

"Over here! Over here!" Eugene called out.

Meredith did a give-and-go with Sally, who passed the ball back, kicking it right past Eugene.

Why won't they kick the ball to me?! What's with them?! Eugene was frustrated. *Wait! Did I accidentally become invisible?!*

Eugene ran down the field, after the two girls, calling out, "I'm right here! I'm right here! I'm just invisible!" But then the stinky stink of something that stunk worse than not being passed the soccer ball filled Eugene's nose.

PEE-YEW!

"Gaaah daaah baaaah waaah!"

The evil sound of nonsense filled Eugene's ears.

There's only one person that can sound that gobbledygooky, Eugene realized.

There! On the sidelines! Queen Stinkypants was at it again! Her stinky diaper of evil was firing across the soccer field and caught Eugene in its awful odor! Not even the soccer fields of Earth were safe from her stink clouds and baby gibberish.

Eugene stopped. It was impossible to run with his lungs filled with Queen Stinkypants Diaper Air. He pinched his nose, squinted his eyes and . . .

BAM!

The next thing Eugene knew he was on the ground, flat on his back, holding his stomach.

OOF!

He'd been hit by the soccer ball. Hard. In the glare of the sun he saw the outline of two faces staring down at him. Two *very* similar faces.

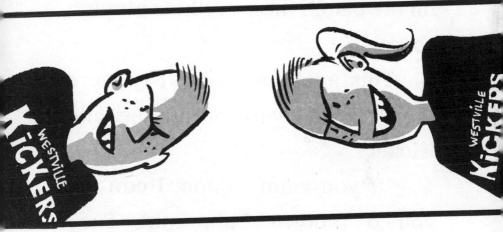

If "mean" could put on a blue jersey and play soccer for ninety minutes on Saturday afternoons, you'd have George and Lulu Morris.

Matching brown hair with pale skin and freckles, they were more like two twin bulldogs chasing an old, slobber-drenched tennis ball on the beach than two kids playing soccer.

This explained why they were the all-star players for the Westville Kickers.

"If you want to nap, I can get you a pillow!" Lulu said. They laughed and ran upfield, dribbling the ball and passing it between them.

Coach McGillicudy called a time-out and ran over to Eugene. "You want to take a break for a little bit, son?" he asked.

Eugene looked up and saw his dad's face. The sun outlined his head like a halo.

"Yeah," Eugene mumbled.

Eugene plopped on the bench next to Bernie Melnick, who had earned a reputation as one of the second grade's greatest benchwarmers.

"It's nice here on the bench, isn't it, Eugene?" Bernie asked. "This is a much nicer bench than the one for basketball, and lots more comfortable than the benches on the baseball field. Yep, for bench-sitting, the soccer field can't be beat!"

Bernie continued, completely unaware that the last thing Eugene wanted to do was to talk.

"You did pretty well against the ready-steady-kick," Bernie said.

"What do you mean?"

"The ready-steady-kick," Bernie replied. "It's the play the Morris twins are famous for. I heard from a friend of a friend of my cousin that the Morris twins once used their ready-steady-kick to knock a guy so far back in time that he became a pirate on a Spanish ship, true story!"

But Eugene didn't have time to think about the impossibility of going back through time from a soccer kick. Eugene was too busy sitting in stunned silence.

Somehow Turbo, the hamster, had rolled his Turbomobile out of Eugene's backpack and was headed into the middle of the soccer action! Turbo rolled under George's feet as he tried to pass the ball to his sister. George tripped over the Turbomobile

and crashed flat on his face.

PLOP!

"Ow! Muh hace! Muh hace!" George's cries were muffled by the grass in his mouth.

George jumped to his feet and spit out a mouthful of turf, totally unaware that Meredith had sped past him. Meredith dribbled downfield dodging the remaining Kickers. Charlie was open, and in a flash she passed the ball across the field.

"Go, Charlie, go!" she yelled. "Take it in!"

Eugene stood on the bench to get a better view. His heart pounded in his chest! This was even better than the time Super Dude scored a touchdown as time ran out to beat the

Halftime Show-Offs in the Super Dude Bowl.

Charlie dribbled toward the goal!

"GO! GO! GO!" Eugene screamed from the bench!

Charlie faked a pass to Marlo, freezing the defender in his tracks, then unleashed a massive kick!

WHAM!

The soccer ball sailed toward the net! The goalie dove! The ball skipped once on the grass and bounced off the fingers of the goalie's outstretched hands!

"GOOOOOOOOOAL!" Eugene shouted and fell off the bench. He jumped to his feet in time to see Turbo scampering for the sidelines.

Way to go, Turbo! Way to go, Nacho Cheese Man! Eugene thought.

The score may have read Westville: 1, Sunnyview: 1, but in Eugene's mind it was Sunnyview Superhero Squad: 1, and Baron and Baroness Von Booger: a huge, big, fat 0.

ZEE-RO!

And the Von Boogers weren't happy about it. The Baron glared at the Turbomobile with laserlike eyes. It was up to Eugene to rescue

his sidekick from the twin terror soccer-ball-kicking feet of the Von Boogers. He leaped from the bench and ran toward his little buddy.

"Get your laser eyes away from my hamster!" Eugene yelled.

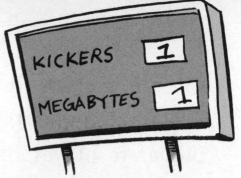

The Westville Kickers: 1, Sunnyview Megabytes: 1.

No matter what planet you were from or what language you spoke when you spoke of these things, there was no denying that the score was tied!

TIED!

And ties were really the only things that were made to be broken. Especially if Sunnyview was going to win its first game of the season.

The Kickers had the ball and brought it upfield, passing it from player to player like it was a hot potato traveling on a rocket.

George had recovered from his horrible "grass-facing" and he kicked the ball to his sister. Evan Mason raced between George and Lulu and tried to steal the ball. The ball hit his shin guards and knocked him over like a bowling pin.

PLOP!

Lulu ran in and dribbled the ball away. She bolted for the Sunnyview goal and passed the ball to Russell Tater. Sally Williams tried to block it.

She was fast. She was fearless. She missed the ball.

Russell passed it to George, and without slowing down, he smacked it with his right foot. It was over almost as soon as it began.

Goal.

SIGH.

Westville: 2, Sunnyview: 1. The tie score was history, thanks to the Morris twins, and Eugene felt a twisting knot in his stomach.

BREET!

And then the whistle blew.

HALFTIME.

The Megabytes headed to the bench, which Eugene and Bernie had been keeping warm for them. Eugene pulled Charlie from the

huddle. "Listen," he whispered to his best friend. "I've had a lot of time to . . . watch . . . the game and I discovered something pretty amazing."

"The soccer ball is a robot that's mind-controlled by the double-brain powers of the Morris twins?!" Charlie asked.

"Yes!" Eugene replied. "I mean, no. I mean, that's what I thought at first too, but then I noticed an ice cooler near their bench—"

Charlie turned to look. "Don't look!" Eugene snapped. "They'll know we're on to them. I saw something like this before in Super Dude No. 26. Super Dude's powers were slowly being sucked away by El-Sucko!, who used a powerful sucking ray hidden in a wedge of stinky blue cheese to rob Super Dude of his powers.

"Baron and Baroness Von

Booger must be using an evil sucking thingie to zap Captain Awesome's awesome powers and make me, I mean him, trip over soccer balls."

Charlie gasped. "That was my *second* guess."

"If Captain Awesome is going to get back into the game and win it, I've gotta destroy whatever evil-sucking machine is in that cooler. It's stealing my powers!"

"What can I do?" Charlie asked.

"I need a distraction."

Before Eugene could say another word, both boys yelled, "Super Sonic Scream!"

"Good luck," Eugene said.

"Same to you," Charlie replied, and took a deep breath. "AAAA AAAAAAAAAAAAAAAAAAA AAAAAAAAAH!" the boy screamed and raced onto the soccer field waving his arms like a crazy duck who'd forgotten how to fly.

But the diversion was perfect! No one saw Captain Awesome superjump across the field and land atop the Westville Kickers' mysterious cooler of icy cold refreshments. . . .

COOL-LAH

KICKERS 2

MEGABYTES 1

"I know we're down two to one," Coach McGillicudy said at halftime. "But I'm really proud of the way you're all playing . . . and . . . um . . . sonic screaming."

That was just one of the many reasons Eugene loved his dad: no matter how busy he might be doing other things, he always made time to give a little look of thanks to his son's efforts to crush evil.

"The Westville Kickers may be

winning, but remember, the game isn't over until the final whistle," Coach McGillicudy continued. "And nobody unplugs the Megabytes!"

"*YEAH!*" Coach McGillicudy led the team in the team cheer that he'd written.

"Megabytes rah!

Megabytes yo!

Megabytes, Megabytes

Yo-ho-ho! High-five!"

The team high-fived.

Thank goodness it wasn't Dinosaur Delmer singing "Monday," Eugene thought.

BREET-TWEET-TWEET!

Halftime was over. Eugene headed back to the bench, but his dad tapped his shoulder.

"You're going the wrong way, Eugene."

"But the bench is that way,"Eugene explained.

"I know, but the soccer field is *that* way. You do want to play, don't you?"

Eugene looked into his dad's eyes and his spirit soared! He gave his dad a quick hug, then raced onto the field, joining Charlie at midfield.

"I really wish I had my cape right now," Eugene whispered.

"I've been thinking about that," Charlie whispered back. "And you know what? That cape isn't Captain Awesome, *you* are. I mean, even without my Nacho Cheese Man outfit, *I* am *still* Nacho Cheese Man. I have all the powers of cheese in a can, not my superhero outfit."

As Eugene watched, Charlie scooted across the field and took control of the ball. "Cheesy-yo!" he yelled.

Nacho Cheese Man's classic battle cry startled the Morris twins, allowing Charlie to break past them and head for the Westville goal.

"Go, Nacho, go!" Eugene yelled and followed after him just in case someone accidentally passed him the ball now that he was no longer invisible.

 Charlie slid his foot under the ball and blasted it into the air. The ball curved! It arced around goalie Bingo Swanson, and bounced into the goal.

YEAH!

Westville: 2, Sunnyview: 2.

TIED!

AGAIN!

But time was running out.

Then a thought shot into Eugene's mind: *Charlie's right! We're not superheroes because we wear superhero outfits! We wear superhero outfits because we're superheroes! I'm Captain Awesome with or without my cape, and I bet if I jumped as high as I can, I'd be able to leap over Baron and Baroness Von Booger and land in front of their goal! Then if anybody would just pass me the ball, it'd be an easy goal!*

Eugene crouched low and jumped as high as he could.

"MI-TEE!" he yelled as his feet left the ground.

The soccer ball
smacked Eugene in
the head.

OUCH!

As Eugene fell to the
ground, it was as if the world
started to move in s-l-o-w
motion. The Megabytes and the
Kickers watched as the soccer ball

arced over the Von Booger twins' evil heads. They tried to block it, but really, who could ever jump as high as Captain Awesome?

The ball hit the ground, bounced once, sailed over Bingo's head and hit the back of the net.

GOOOOOOOAAAAAL!

BREET-TWEET-TWEET!

The clock ran out! The referee blew his whistle! The soccer game was over, and the Megabytes had won, 3–2!

"You did it, Eugene," Coach McGillicudy said, as he ran onto the field. "You scored the winning goal!"

"MI-TEE!" Charlie said, which made Eugene's smile even bigger.

"Nice going, Eugene!"

Did Meredith really say something nice to me?! Wow. She even used my real name? That ball must've hit me so hard I'm hearing

things! Eugene thought and rubbed his head.

The Megabytes raised Eugene on their shoulders and carried him off the field. The Morris twins stood in front of their goal, arms folded.

They were too stunned to move, or maybe they were waiting for their laser eyes to recharge.

It really didn't matter to Eugene either way. He was filled with a joy and happiness that couldn't be melted, even by the most zaptastic of lasers.

But there was still one more thing for Eugene to do. He had to keep the game ball out of the hands of the Von Boogers. That prize now belonged to Captain Awesome and his Megabytes, and he wasn't going to let anyone steal it from them.

"Come on, Nacho Cheese Man!" Captain Awesome yelled. "We've got one more goal to tend!" Captain

Awesome and Nacho Cheese Man ran toward the goal where the Von Boogers and the game ball waited. . . .

YUM!

The best th about soccer, though, isn't the winning. It's going out for pizza after a game. Coach McGillicudy treated all the Megabytes to Jumbo Everything Pizzas from Jumbo's Pizza Palace.

Evan, Sally, Bernie, Meredith,

Mike, Marlo, and Charlie all agreed that Eugene would get the slice that had the most pepperoni.

And not only that, but Eugene managed to avoid the salad bar and not eat any of the green stuff.

Does life get any better?

Yes, it does.

Because on the drive home, Eugene's dad forgot to play any Dinosaur Delmer songs.

Both boys were eager to return to their neighborhood. They'd been gone for nearly two hours. Who knew how much eviling evil had been doing in their absence? Perhaps some horrible mutant monster from the sewer had gotten loose and started knocking over mailboxes or digging holes in people's yards.

"BUT"—Eugene began—"if there is no evil to be found . . . I mean, if EVERYTHING is absolutely, totally, completely normal, let's squeeze in a little soccer practice before our next Sunnyview Superhero Squad meeting."

"You took the cheese right out of my can!" Charlie replied.

MI-TEE!

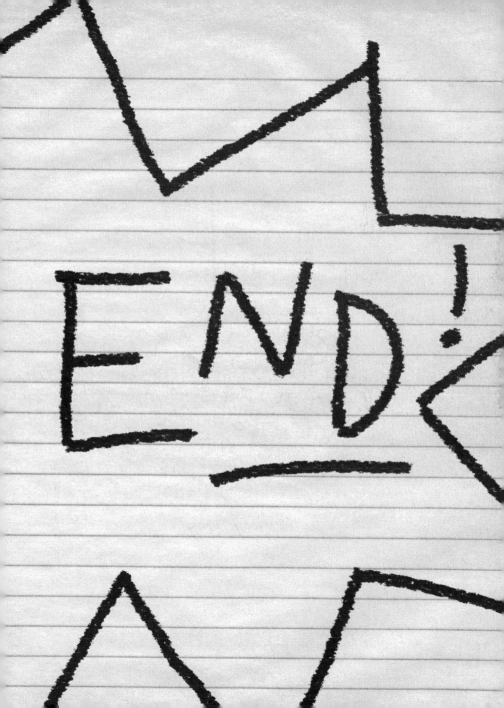

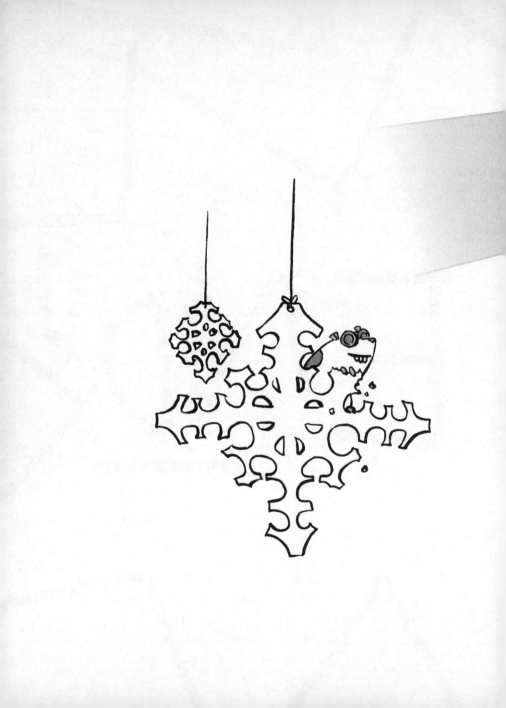

Table of Contents

TING!
TINGGG!
TINGGGGG!

"I love to play the triangle!" Eugene McGillicudy yelled out in a very heroic voice. In Mrs. Randle's music class, Eugene always went for the triangle. "I like any musical instrument that's shaped like a slice of pizza!"

SHAKE!
SHAKE-SHAKE!

"Keep your triangle,"
said Eugene's best friend,
Charlie Thomas Jones. "I like
the maracas. I don't know what's
inside, but I hope it's dried bugs."

SHAKE!

Every Thursday morning, Sunnyview Elementary School's music teacher, Mrs. Randle, passed out an assortment of xylophones, tambourines, recorders, cowbells, bongo drums, and more to all the second graders in her music room.

Eager students from different classes grabbed them like free chocolate, and sang and played under Mrs. Randle's waving baton.

"Cowbell!" cried Evan Mason as he grabbed one from the stack.

"I'm getting the tambourine!" yelled Meredith Mooney, dressed in pink, from the ribbons in her hair to the shoelaces in her pink shoes. She had secretly stuck pink tape on the tambourine to mark it her own.

Then Colin Boyle, who was from Mrs. Duncan's second-grade class, grabbed a set of bongo drums. **_BAMMITY-BAM! BAM!_**

He bammed them with the palms of his hands. "Nice," he said.

"Okay, class," Mrs. Randle said. "Let's get started."

"And a one, and a two, and a one, two, three, four," she called, swinging her baton like she was swatting at a lazy fly.

Eugene tinged and Charlie shook, because superheroes who step in front of danger aren't afraid to make as much crazy loud music as possible. Just like that time Super Dude fought his musical enemy, Trouble Clef, and knocked the musical scales right off his slide trombone.

KA-PUNCH!

What's that?

You've never heard of Super Dude? Really?! Have you never been to a comic book store? Do you not watch cartoons on television? Do you not have the limited edition Super Dude Wristwatch?

Super Dude was absolutely the greatest superhero ever— he was also the star of a number of comic books. Eugene had boxes of them under his bed. And in his

closet. And stacked in the corner. Following Super Dude's example, Eugene created his own costume and became . . .

TA-DA!

CAPTAIN AWESOME!

Along with his best friend, Charlie, also known as the super-hero Nacho Cheese Man, he formed the Sunnyview Superhero Squad to stop evil from eviling in Sunnyview.

This was good because Eugene and Charlie lived in Sunnyview and there was a surprising amount of eviling going on.

But so far, at least for today, Charlie and Eugene hadn't seen any bad guys at Sunnyview Elementary School—just the happy, loud sounds of a triangle and a set of maracas.

TING!

SHAKE!

TINGGG!

SHAKE-SHAKE!

"Can we please stop all that noise?" asked the awful My! Me! Mine! Mere-DITH Mooney. The pink ribbons in her hair were tied in perfect bows. Her pink bows were perfect like the grades she expected on her report card.

Meredith had a lot of rules and one of them was about noise. "Noise," she always said to Eugene, "is noisy. And I doubt there's anything more noisy than *you*."

I'll bet she thinks it'll wrinkle all that pink, Eugene thought.

"Mrs. Randle, I can't concentrate on my tambourine if Barfgene and Charlie Thomas Bonehead keep making those awful sounds."

SHAKE!

"Is she talking about us?" Charlie whispered to Eugene.

TING!

"Bad guys always complain about superheroes," Eugene whispered back. Meredith was not only the pink Mooney who complained about everything, but she was also Captain Awesome's archenemy, Little Miss Stinky Pinky!

"Little Miss Stinky Pinky's trying to stop our Anti-Evil Symphony!" Charlie said.

"Well, that's what *she* thinks!" Eugene replied. "No evil is going to knock the notes off our scales today!"

"**C**lass, I have a special announcement to make," Mrs. Randle said.

A special announcement? Eugene *loved* special announcements.

"It's something very special," she added.

Very special announcements are even better, Eugene thought.

"Is the school going to be

turned into a rocket ship and blast
off for Altair's green sun where all
of my friends can get superpowers?" Eugene asked hopefully.

"Ummm .. no . . . ," Mrs. Randle
said.

"Is the school going to be turned
into the new headquarters for the
League of Superheroes for Justice?"
Charlie asked.

Mrs. Randle shook her head. "Not quite, Charlie."

Then it must be something really, awesomely superly biggish! Eugene thought.

"I know!" he called out. "The school's going to be turned into a giant science lab that takes zombie dinosaurs and turns them into *super* zombie dinosaurs!"

But no, that wasn't right, either.

"Before we go on winter break," Mrs. Randle said, "we'll be perform-ing our holiday play: *The Winter Wonderland!*"

Eugene and Charlie looked at each other.

"I thought you said it was some-thing very special?" Eugene asked.

"It *is* very special!" Mrs. Randle

replied. "It's going to be a wonder-land of winter." She was so excited it was like she was jumping out of her shoes.

"Don't worry, Mrs. Randle. I'll star in the play for you," Meredith volunteered.

"Everyone will get a chance to participate," Mrs. Randle said. "Tryouts are on Monday. There will be songs, music, dancing, holiday lights, everything you need to make a wonderland!"

Songs and performances . . . in front of an audience . . . at school . . . at night?! Eugene's mind was twirling. *Maybe this* is *better than super zombie dinosaurs.*

"There'll be three rehearsals after school," Mrs. Randle said. "You guys have to be ready for your big stage debuts."

"I'm ready right now!" Eugene said. "Listen!" He *TINGED* his triangle again as hard as he could.

TINGGGGG!

"That's really great, Eugene."
Mrs. Randle's ears were ringing.
"But you can sign up for the tryouts
here." She pointed to the clipboard
on her desk.

SCAMPER!

PUSH!

SHOVE!

PLAY TRYOUT SIGN-UP

"Make way!"

"Me first!"

"Where's that pencil?"

Everyone rushed to the sign-up
sheet to list the parts they wanted
to try out for. Eugene and Charlie
shot each other a look. They knew

instantly where they wanted to be.

"Are you thinking what I'm thinking, Charlie?"

"You bet I am," he said.

"Snowflake Symphony!" they said at the same time.

"We'll be able to see the whole auditorium!" Eugene said. "As Captain Awesome and Nacho Cheese Man, we can keep an eye out for Sunnyview's major villains."

"No evil badness will sabotage our holiday play!" Charlie said.

But badness was already in the room. Who were all these people blocking their way to the clipboard? This was not a classroom filled with happy children, this was really the Evil Student Mutant League!

And they were out to stop Captain Awesome and Nacho Cheese Man from joining the Snowflake Symphony! Well, not today!

"Step aside, Evil Student Mutants!" Captain Awesome said.

In!

On Monday, Eugene's audition was super.

"MI-TEE!" he yelled. "I'm in the Snowflake Symphony! As lead triangle! Look out, Winter Wonderland! My Triangle of Justice shall ring loud this day!"

TING! TING! TING!

"Cheesy-YO!" Charlie said. "I'm in, too! Mrs. Randle said I shook the maracas like the best maracas-shaker she'd ever seen!"

SHAKE-SHAKE-SHAKE!

Evan Mason was next for his audition. He did a very dramatic performance as a snowflake.

"Today, I am a snowflake," Evan said. "Watch as I fall gently from the sky, landing safely on the ground, as quiet as a whisper. *Then!*" His voice became more dramatic. "I'm scooped up by a snowplow, scraped into a pile of snow by the side of the road, and mashed into a giant snow fort. The end!"

Next, Sally Williams did her impression of Super Snowball, the world's greatest snow-powered superhero. "I am Super Snowball!" she yelled in a very heroic voice. "No evil shall escape from my slushy snowballs!"

Sally ran around the

music room throwing imaginary snowballs at invisible villains. "Slush attack! Your crime is no match for my anti-evil snowballs!"

Wow! Sally can really fight evil, Eugene thought.

But it was Mike Flinch who really impressed Eugene—and everyone else in the class—with his song.

"Snowman, snowman, wonderland.

In the snow globe in my hand.

If I shake you left and right,

Will you be dizzy day and night?

Snowman, snowman, wonderland!"

BRAVO!

Everyone in the class applauded. Mrs. Randle rushed to Mike and shook his hand.

"I think we've found our lead," she said. "Class, Mike will star as the Sunnyview Snowman in *The Winter Wonderland!*"

HOORAY!

Everyone knew how important that role was. Ted Lee was last year's Sunnyview Snowman and he went on to play the Cactus King in the Spring Pageant! Mike had big shoes to fill.

"Way to go, Mike!" Eugene and Charlie cheered.

"Uh . . . I'd like to thank my

Uncle Lewis for teaching me everything I know about show tunes," Mike said. The only thing bigger than Mike's smile was the big, round white snowman head he'd be wearing as his snowman costume.

"Yeah, yeah, that's great, hooray and all for Mike," Meredith said. "But let's get to the really big news. What star part do I get to play?"

Mrs. Randle flipped through the notes on her clipboard. "You get to play the Icy Icicle in the Frozen Chorus!"

"What?!" she yelled. "What?!" she repeated. "What?!" she said again. "The Icy Icicle is *not* the star! It's just an *icicle*! What kind of play stars an *icicle*?! None! I should be the star!"

The pink ribbons in Meredith's hair shook so

hard that one of them popped out. She stomped off to the girls' bathroom to repair her pinkness.

Charlie and Eugene smiled at each other. What a great day!

"*The Winter Wonderland* is only a few weeks away," Mrs. Randle said. "After-school practices will be on the next two Thursdays from three-thirty to five p.m. Please let your parents know and have them sign your permission slips."

YAY!

"No homework on Thursday nights!" Eugene cheered.

"Oh no," Mrs. Randle corrected. "You'll still have to do your homework, but *Winter Wonderland* practice will be fun!"

BOO! Still have to do homework?! How is that fun?! Eugene wondered.

Some fun it was, if the dreaded Homework Monster from Planet Textbook was still assigning evil assignments! Enough was enough! It was time for Captain Awesome and Nacho Cheese Man to fight against the Homework Monster's unfair Study Bombs.

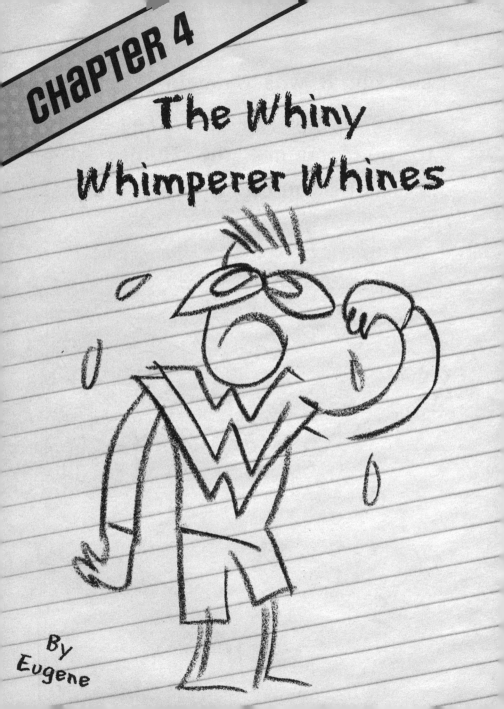

"I can see everything!" Eugene exclaimed, standing in the back row with the rest of the Snowflake Symphony.

"Do you have super vision too?" Charlie asked.

Eugene shook his head. "No, but I have the perfect seat to watch out for evil."

It was Thursday after school and all the *Winter Wonderland* performers arrived for their first rehearsal. While they stumbled around looking for their assigned seats, Eugene and Charlie were already sitting in theirs.

"It's good to get here early," Eugene said.

"Evil doesn't rest, even during rehearsals!" Charlie agreed.

"Evil doesn't stand a chance," Eugene said. "The citizens of Sunnyview have nothing to worry about with Captain Awesome and Nacho Cheese Man on the job."

TAP!

TAP!

TAP!

Eugene's anti-evil declarations were interrupted when Mrs. Randle tapped her baton against the music stand.

"Instruments...ready!"

she called out. "And a one, and a two, and a one, two, three, four!"

The Snowflake Symphony started to play the *Winter Wonderland* music. Eugene and Charlie played their instruments as loud as possible.

TING! TING! TING! SHAKE! SHAKE! SHAKE!

But then a hand shot up from the orchestra. "Mrs. Randle!" the hand called out.

Eugene traced the hand to Jake Story, a second-grader who was in Mrs. Martin's class. Jake stood up. He had red hair that was slicked back like bright red string. He was wearing a tie.

A TIE!

Who wears a tie to school? Eugene wondered.

And who keeps it on after school?

"Mrs. Randle, oh yoo-hoo! Mrs. Randle!" Jake called out.

"Yes, Jake?"

"I can't play *my* triangle because Eugene is banging on his way too loud," Jake said. "It's hurting my ears! And I *do* get ear infections . . ."

"Very well," Mrs. Randle said. "I have the perfect solution."

Mrs. Randle did have the perfect solution. For evil. She not only moved Eugene far away from Jake, but also from Charlie. Worse, Eugene's view of the audience was now blocked by branches from the giant snow-covered tree on the stage.

As Eugene grumbled in his new seat, he and Charlie shared a knowing look—the kind of all-knowing look that superheroes share whenever they realize there's a bad guy right in the room with them raising its evil hand and complaining about "ear infections."

This "Jake Story" from "Mrs. Martin's class" was clearly up to no good. For this was no ordinary second-grader! Jake was really **The Whiny Whimperer**, a constant complainer determined to keep Captain Awesome and Nacho Cheese Man apart. If that was true, he was in for an awesome surprise!

But fear not! Captain Awesome and Nacho Cheese Man would not be separated by evil whining!

"Class, I have a terrible announcement to make."

Oh no! Eugene thought. *Terrible announcements are always terrible!*

"Let me guess: Our principal is really an alien invader from the Planet Do-What-I-Tell-You?!" Eugene asked.

Mrs. Randle chuckled. "You have a wild imagination, Eugene, but alien invaders would be good news today."

If alien invaders were good news, what could possibly be the bad news?

Eugene looked around for evil, but his Captain Awesome Evil-Detection Powers detected nothing out of the ordinary. "But Mrs. Randle, everything is where it should be. No one's taken the glittery pinecones.

The fake snowflakes are still in their boxes and even the Sunnyview Snowman costume is on its hook."

How bad can it be?

BAD.

"It seems that poor Mike Flinch has gotten the flu and will no longer be able to be the Sunnyview Snowman in the play," Mrs. Randle sadly informed the students.

"Oh, my," Meredith said, very dramatically. "Poor Mike! Poor, poor

Mike! Whatever will we do without him!" She pressed the back of her hand to her forehead like she was going to faint. "Looks like you'll need the best actor remaining to play the snowman," Meredith said, trying her hardest to be the best actor.

"Oh, I know what we can do—" Eugene started to say.

"So do I, Eww-Gene, so do I," Meredith interrupted. "*The Winter Wonderland* needs someone to come in and save the day. The play needs someone who can be the Sunnyview Snowman and make the Winter Wonderland a true wonder of winter." She looked at Mrs. Randle with really big eyes, "Tell me, Mrs. Randle, who will play the Snowman now and save our Wonderland?"

BARF! Could anyone be more barfier than Meredith?

"Thank you, Meredith, for that very dramatic performance, but you are perfect for the Icy Icicle."

"But I only have *one* line, Mrs. Randle!" Meredith protested. "'Brrrr . . . it's cold even for an icicle like me.' I could say it in my sleep."

"And you say it so well, dear," Mrs. Randle said. "Besides, after careful consideration, I've made my choice. The student playing the Sunnyview Snowman will be . . . **Eugene McGillicudy!**"

Mrs. Randle announced.

Poor kid, Eugene thought, looking around to see if he could spot the miserable expression on the doomed student's face. *Stuck looking like he's wearing a white bowling ball on his head while he sings with Meredith Moo— BY THE BARF IN MY MOUTH! EUGENE MCGILLICUDY?! THAT'S ME!*

"Aaaaaaaaaaaaaaaaaaaaaaaaah! I don't want to wear a white bowling ball on my head!"

"Oh, Eugene!" Mrs. Randle replied. "The snowman's head isn't a white bowling ball. It's a white *plastic* ball . . . with holes for eyes." She snapped the large, white ball on Eugene's head.

"You look like you're wearing a marshmallow helmet," Charlie whispered. "Like Marshy the Evil

Marshmallow King from Super Dude No. 56."

"Come on, Eugene. You're in the front row, now. Right next to Meredith."

The walk from the back row to the front row, where he would be beside a fuming icicle in pink ribbons, was only fifteen feet, but to Eugene it felt like he was walking a billion miles with a marshmallow helmet on his head.

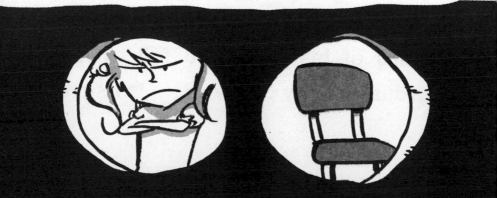

Eugene slid in next to Meredith. He had to get out of the front row. *I'll never be able to see any villains from here!*

Eugene knew he couldn't tell Mrs. Randle the truth. He couldn't let anyone know he was really Captain Awesome. So he came up with the next best excuse.

"Mrs. Randle! The marshmallow helmet has brain-sucking eels inside! They're sucking out my braaaaaains!" Eugene grabbed the sides of his head and fell to the ground. "Only . . . way . . . to save me . . . is to move me . . . into the . . . back row . . . again."

Mrs. Randle stared at Eugene, slightly annoyed. "Eugene. It's *not* a marshmallow helmet. It's the head of the Sunnyview Snowman, but if you think you can do a better job, then you can make the snowman's costume next year."

"Braaaaaaaaains . . ." Eugene gurgled and squirmed on the floor.

"I think someone is just acting out because they're nervous about being the snowman . . . ," Mrs. Randle said.

"I'd be nervous, too, if I danced like Eubean." Meredith snorted.

"Let's make a promise to each other, Eugene." Mrs. Randle helped him up from the floor. "I promise that I'll help you to be a GREAT snowman. And you promise me that you'll stop ruining my costumes."

Eugene felt the side of his

head. Rolling around had dented the side of the Styrofoam helmet. *Great. Now I'm going to be a block-head snowman.*

Eugene sighed. There was no way out. He would have to sing and dance with an angry pink Popsicle, and Charlie would have to be on villain patrol alone.

"Deal," Eugene finally replied, knowing exactly how Super Dude felt when he had to disguise himself as a turnip to save the Cauliflower Kid from the steamy Cabbage Patch in Super Dude No. 12 *Special Vegetarian Edition.*

"Okay, my little snowflakes and icicles and snowmen and all you other wintry things, let's try the play's dance finale, 'Jingle Bells'!" Mrs. Randle called out.

"Dashing through the snow, in a one course soapy day!" Eugene's warbly voice warbled while he counted "One, two, three" in his head to keep his dancing feet in

time with Meredith's. But when
Meredith spun left, Eugene spun
right and . . .

DANCE!

TRIP!

PINECONE!

Eugene crashed into Philip Fernbottom who was dressed as a winter pinecone. Then Philip stumbled and fell into Sonia DeRosa, a snow-flake, who bumped into Charlie and caused the whole row of snowflakes

to topple like white, glittery dominoes.

The music stopped as kids in various winter costumes rolled on their backs and waved their arms like overturned turtles.

"I don't even know where to

start," Meredith started. "*First* of all, what does 'One course soapy day' even mean?"

"How should I know?" Eugene defended. "I didn't write the song."

"It's 'One *horse open sleigh*,' Eubean," Meredith corrected. "And you spun right when you were supposed to spin left. You *do* know the difference between left and right, right?"

"*Yeah*," Eugene replied. He stood silently with his arms crossed, but then realized everyone was staring. "Left! See!" he snapped,

raising his left hand.

"That'll show her!" Charlie whispered, waddling on the ground near Eugene's feet, waiting for someone to help him stand up.

CHAPTER 6

Chilly with a Slight
Chance of Evil!

By
Eugene

"Any play rehearsal that ends with Meredith mad at you can't be all that bad," Charlie offered as the two boys walked home after school.

Eugene felt happy to be out of the snow-man costume.

"I don't know why Mrs. Randle picked me to be the snowman," Eugene sighed, small white sparkles falling from his ear. "I can't sing or dance and the snowman is the most important part of the play!"

"I know! I don't know what Mrs. Randle was thinking!" Charlie laughed until he saw Eugene glaring at him. "I mean . . . I don't know what Mrs. Randle was thinking . . . when she . . . made that snowman costume."

"And the worst part is, I have to dance with My! Me! Mine! Mere-DITH!" Eugene groaned. "Oh, Charlie, why would Mrs. Randle do this to me?"

A light went off in Charlie's head. "That's it! There's no better place to watch for the bad guys than center stage!"

"You're right!" Eugene replied. "I'll bet Mrs. Randle is a double undercover secret spy sent to help us defeat the evil bad stuff that evil does!"

"This calls for a Double Nacho Cheese Celebration!" Charlie cheered. He slid off his backpack  and pulled out a can of nacho cheese.

EMPTY!

"Cheesy underwear! I'm out!" Charlie said in disbelief. "Do you have my backup can?"

"Don't I always?" Eugene reached inside his backpack, but something besides Charlie's canned cheese awaited within.

"It's a note . . ." Eugene showed the crayon-scrawled paper to Charlie.

"'Ice to meet you. My name is Mr. Chill,'" Charlie read, his eyes wide. "'If you had cold feet at the rehearsal today, you'll really get the

big freeze tomorrow if
you don't quit the play. Catch
my *drift*? PS This is snow joke.'"

"Someone wants me to quit the
play? But who?" Eugene asked.

"I'll bet it was Meredith!"
Charlie gasped.

"Impossible!" Eugene said, studying the note. "Her writing is way nicer than this and she'd have little hearts and butterflies and pink unicorns with wings drawn all over it."

Both boys stood in silence imagining the horrors of an evil note threatening to put the "big freeze" on Eugene, covered in hearts and butterflies and pink unicorns with wings.

"That's just gross," Charlie said.

Time passed. Hours turned into days and days turned into more days. Eugene practiced every day. He sang. He danced. He counted in his head. And then a very strange thing happened.

"Oh, what fun, it is to ride, in a one . . . horse . . . o-pen sleiiiiiiigh!"

Eugene sang the song perfectly. He didn't knock down a single winter pinecone or snowflake *or* the

angry, pink Icicle. He raised his little snowman arms into the air and belted out the last words of "Jingle Bells."

Mrs. Randle was right. He *could* do this.

As the song ended, Eugene the Snowman stood perfectly still. The snowflakes of Sunnyview gathered around him and carefully placed decorations on his snowman costume.

"And as the snowflakes place the decorations on you, *that's* when you say the last line of the play, "'Snow glad you could all come. Happy holidays!'" Mrs. Randle said.

But Eugene wasn't listening. He was doing something much more important. His eyes scanned the faces of his fellow *Winter Wonderland* performers.

Who wrote that note? he wondered. *Which one of you wants me out of the play?*

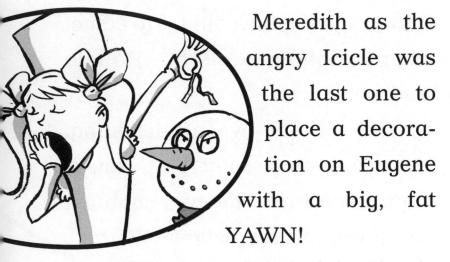

Meredith as the angry Icicle was the last one to place a decoration on Eugene with a big, fat YAWN!

"That was wonderful! Simply wonderful!" Mrs. Randle gushed. "And Eugene...you were marvelous."

Eugene didn't reply. His cheeks turned red, and he stared at the ground.

"But Meredith, my dear . . ." Mrs. Randle continued, "the end is supposed to be a celebration. You looked so . . . bored."

"Don't you worry," grumpy Meredith said to Mrs. Randle. "When that curtain rises on opening night, I'll bring it."

As Mrs. Randle continued giving tips to the rest of the students, Eugene gave a thumbs-up to Charlie.

SNEAK!

ZIP!

SUPERHERO!

Within seconds,
the boys were backstage digging
their superhero outfits from their
backpacks.

"Over here!" Captain Awesome
whispered.

Nacho Cheese Man grabbed
a can of hot dog–flavored cheese
and crept with Captain Awesome

behind a large dressing mirror.

"We can hide back here and watch my backpack!" Captain Awesome explained in an awesome, yet still very whispery voice.

And then—as Nacho Cheese Man took the first suck of flavored canned cheese—THEY SAW IT!

A HAND!

WITH A NOTE!

REACHING FOR EUGENE'S BACKPACK!

"Mun mand mat matmack!"
Nacho Cheese Man leapt from
behind the large mirror and
shouted, his tongue sticking to the
roof of his mouth.

"Freeze or face Captain
Awesome's One–Two Spinning
Punch!" Captain Awesome called
out. He spun around and around,

his arms extended like blades of a helicopter.

The hand dropped the note! Running footsteps echoed!

Captain Awesome spun in two more circles, staggered forward and tripped over his backpack.

"Whoa . . . dizzy . . . too much whirlwinding . . ."

"Mall met mim!" Nacho Cheese Man said, trying desperately to unstick his tongue from the roof of his mouth.

Then, something moved! The heroes spun and faced a walking pinecone!

"AAAAAAAAH!" they both screamed before realizing it was just Philip Fernbottom.

"Whoa," Philip said. "Are you guys in the play?"

"Yes! In the 'play' of Good versus Evil!" Captain Awesome replied. "But there's no singing or dancing. There's

only the crushing of evil beneath my Superhero Sneakers."

Philip Fernbottom took one look at himself dressed as a giant pinecone and said, "I wanna be in *your* play."

But it was too late. Captain Awesome and Nacho Cheese Man were gone. Into the back wings of the stage they raced! Something moved again! This time it wasn't a pinecone. Someone was behind the giant cardboard candy cane leaning against the wall . . . and it sure wasn't one of Santa's elves.

Nacho Cheese Man ran to the other side of the candy cane, cutting off all hope of escape for the cowering bad guy.

"Show your face, if you dare!" Captain Awesome said.

A boy stood up from behind the candy cane prop.

"The Whiney Whimperer?!" Captain Awesome and Nacho Cheese Man gasped in unison.

"Why can't you call me 'Mr. Chill?'" Jake Story whined.

"I don't like being called 'The Whiney Whimperer.'"

"Sorry, villain, but *we* get to name the bad guys, not you," Captain Awesome replied. "That's just what goodness does!"

"And the other thing goodness does is to find out who you're working for!" Nacho Cheese Man called out as the two heroes rushed into action!

"CHEESY-YO!" "MI-TEE!"

CHAPTER 8

Jake and the Stampeding Elephant

By Eugene

"**I** only wanted Eugene to quit the play so I could be the star," Jake confessed. His red, greased-back hair made it look like he had orange jam smeared all over his head. "*I'm* a better triangle player than he is *and* a better dancer! Watch!"

Jake danced. Sort of. He looked more like a puppet flopping about after some of his strings had been cut. He did a final spin and crashed into Nacho Cheese Man.

"Okay, so, maybe I need to work on that part a little bit more, but I'm still a better triangle player!" Jake whined.

"The only thing you're better at is making my ears hurt," Captain Awesome replied. "Now, who else is in on your chilly plan of evil?!"

"Yeah! Who *are* you with?!" Nacho Cheese Man snapped. "I'll bet it's Dr. Spinach! Or Queen Stinkypants!"

"No one! I don't even know who Queen Spinach and Dr. Stinkypants are! Honest!" Jake claimed. "I was just tired of Eugene getting all the attention. It's just like at home. No one *ever* pays attention to me."

With all that bright red hair on Jake's head, Captain Awesome found it hard to believe at first, but then he thought about the times that his own parents hovered over Molly and he felt totally forgotten.

He could be playing a trumpet on the back of a stampeding elephant crashing cymbals with its trunk and the only reaction his parents would have would be "Oooo! Molly just made a stinky in

her diaper! Who's our little stinky stinkpot?"

Captain Awesome knew that his parents would never, ever really forget him, but sometimes that's still how he *felt*.

Sometimes.

"Please don't tell Mrs. Randle!" Jake pleaded. "I don't want to be kicked out of the play!"

"Don't worry, Jake," Captain Awesome said, calling the boy by his real name. "Your secret is safe with Captain Awesome and Nacho Cheese Man."

"Yeah! And that's what you get for going up against Captain Awesome and—" Nacho Cheese Man threw a confused look to Captain Awesome. "Wait. Did you just say 'your secret is safe?'"

"Yes, Nacho Cheese Man. Safe. If there's one thing Super Dude taught us, it's that sometimes you gotta kick evil in the butt, sometimes you gotta punch evil in the face, but sometimes what you really need to do is . . . help. Like Super Dude says, it's the job of a true hero to know the difference."

"Cheesy-yo . . . ," Nacho Cheese Man whispered in a voice mixed with wonder and admiration. "And that's one more reason why they call him 'Super Dude . . .'"

Captain Awesome turned from his crime-fighting friend and extended his hand to Jake.

"**I think I'm gonna puke!**"
Eugene groaned.

Charlie took a big step to the left. "You'll be fine," he said, then took another step away just to be safe.

"But everyone in the world is out there!" Eugene replied. He peeked through the curtain to see the school auditorium packed with parents and families.

"It's opening night! How's my little snowman doing?" Mrs. Randle asked.

"I think I'm gonna puke!" Eugene groaned.

Mrs. Randle took a big step to the left. "You'll be fine," she said, then took another step away just to be safe.

It was finally the night of the play! The curtain rose to thunderous applause. The snowflakes shuffled out to the main stage.

"Go get 'em!" Jake whispered to Eugene as he passed.

Charlie added, "You'll do great!"

The music started. Eugene waited in the wings for his cue.

GURGLE!

His stomach was going on a roller-coaster ride around his heart.

LOOP!

Then it was in his nose.

ZOOM!

Then it took a twisting turn down to his knees.

And then, just as Eugene's stomach was rocketing down to his ankles, he caught a glimpse of himself in the dressing mirror.

He wasn't just wearing a giant marshmallow suit with a bright red scarf. He was wearing a *costume*. Yes, he looked like a little cloud with sneakers float- ing behind a red curtain, but it was still a costume he was wearing . . .

Just like my Captain Awesome outfit . . . , Eugene realized.

And suddenly his stomach's wild ride slowed down just a little bit. Then as Eugene calmed, a horrible "waaah!" of horribleness filled his ears!

"WAAAAAH!" a voice cried out from the audience.

I'd know that waaahing waaah waah anywhere! Eugene thought and yanked back the curtain.

And there she was! His most

stinky of enemies!

QUEEN STINKYPANTS!

But what was she doing *here*?!

Maybe she just wants to see me sing and dance, Eugene wondered. *Even villains have been known to enjoy a nice winter play. . . .*

What am I thinking?! Eugene said to himself. *My snowman helmet must be on too tight! Queen Stinkypants can only be here for one reason . . . TO MAKE SURE THIS PLAY STINKS!*

But there was no time to change into his Captain Awesome

outfit. Eugene had to stop Queen Stinkypants from ruining the play! Every parent had one arm in the air, recording their kids with their smartphones. A hundred childhood memories would be forever ruined by the stinky stink of Stinkypants!

"The show must go on!" Eugene the Snowman shouted and rushed onto the stage!

CHAPTER 10

A Surprise Star

By
Eugene

CHEERS!
APPLAUSE!
HOORAY!

The play was perfect, filled with laughs, smiles and 152 individual smartphone cameras. And the strangest thing? It was all a blur for Eugene. His snowman instincts took over, and he danced and sang like he'd been doing the same thing every night for his entire life.

Even Meredith the Icy Icicle did a great job. When she told Mrs. Randle not to worry about her once the curtain went up, she wasn't kidding.

Eugene the Snowman and Meredith the Icicle went into the final moves of their dance. Eugene raised his arms and the snow-flakes gathered round with their decorations.

And then an idea came to Eugene. He stepped forward from the group and looked directly at the audience. Time for the last line

of the play. All the smartphones focused on Eugene, except for the one being held by Meredith's mom. Meredith had given her a strict *no-close-ups-on-anyone-but-me* order, and Mrs. Mooney was not about to break it.

"Thank you for coming," Eugene began, "But no Sunnyview celebration would be complete without a word from a very special snowflake . . ."

The auditorium was completely silent except for the ruffling of pages as Mrs. Randle stood in the wings desperately searching through the script to find the lines Eugene was saying.

Eugene coughed. Nothing. Charlie coughed. Nothing. Eugene and Charlie coughed again together. Still nothing. Meredith rolled her eyes, half annoyed and half afraid the two boys would point at her and start shouting their usual "nonsense" about Ms. Pinky

Stinky or Dinky Pinky or whatever it was they always called her.

"Are you okay?" Jake whispered to Eugene.

"Dude, I'm talking about *you*," Eugene whispered back. "Go on . . . say the last line . . . "

Jake paused for a moment, unsure he was hearing Eugene correctly.

He was.

The only thing bigger than Jake's eyes was his smile. He stepped forward into the spotlight. Every smartphone in the audience focused on Jake. Even Mrs. Mooney "accidentally" (as she would explain to her very grumpy daughter hours later when Meredith watched the video at home) zoomed in ever-so-slightly on Jake.

"Snow glad you could all come," he said. "Happy holidays!"

Applause exploded from the audience as everyone stood to cheer Jake and all the performers . . . and no one cheered louder than the first row, filled with two red-headed parents and six red-headed brothers and sisters, who at that moment, were very much paying total attention to their son and brother.

MI-TEE!

"Sometimes, what you really need to do is help," Charlie the Snowflake whispered to Eugene the Snowman.

"That is snow true, Charlie," Eugene answered. "Snow true . . ."

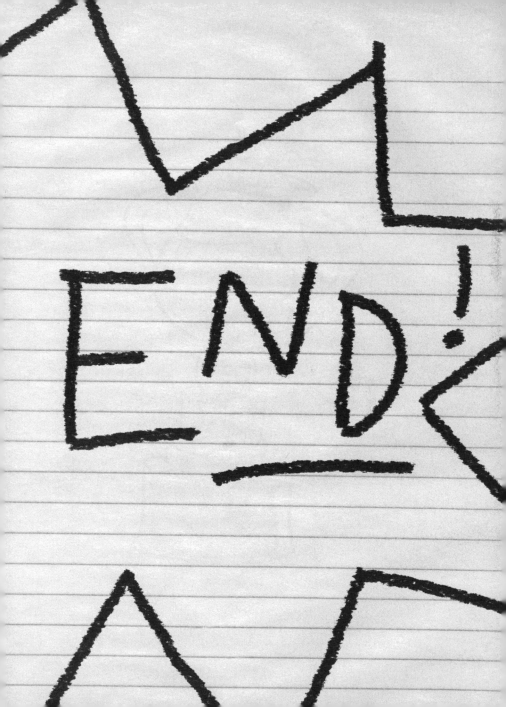

Table of Contents

A-CHOOO! SNIFF! SNURFFLE!

Eugene McGillicudy sat at his desk in Ms. Beasley's class and wiped his nose with a tissue. It was only ten o'clock, and he'd been sneezing all morning.

A-CHOO!

He did it again. Maybe Eugene shouldn't have moved his desk next

to the open window. But he had to. It was the only way Eugene could keep an eye out for evil while still in school.

It was the kind of thing that Super Dude did when he went undercover in *Super Dude vs. the Evil School* No. 2.

What's that?

You've never heard of Super Dude? Really?! How could you not know about the greatest superhero in the whole world? He's the superhero who single-handedly crushed The Crimson Crusher and still had enough time to rescue a baby ferret from an apple tree.

Eugene could tell you all about Super Dude because Eugene had read *every* *single* comic book starring the superhero. In fact, Super Dude was the reason Eugene became Captain Awesome.

With his best friend, Charlie Thomas Jones (also known as the superhero Nacho Cheese Man), and the class pet hamster, Turbo, Eugene formed the Sunnyview Superhero Squad to stop evil bad guys.

Eugene took a deep, happy breath. There was no evil outside the school window today. Then he let out a giant sneeze.

A-CHOOO!

"Dude, you've been sneezing all morning," Charlie whispered. "You okay?"

Charlie was right! Eugene *had*

been sneezing all morning and so had many of the other kids in class.

"Don't you see, Charlie?! It's all part of his evil plan!" Eugene whispered urgently.

"You're right!" Charlie gasped. Then he paused and added, "Whose evil plan?"

"Only the most evil of springtime villains!" Eugene replied. **"The Pollinator!"**

Released from the cold fingers of winter justice, the Pollinator had returned! Dressed in his protective bee suit, he was unleashing the power of uncontrollable sneezing, watery eyes, and stuffy noses!

"This is a job for Captain Awesome and Nacho Cheese Man!" Captain Awesome yelled as he looked out the window. "Get ready, Pollinator! I'm going to wipe your evil nose with the Tissue of Goodness!"

MI-TEE!

"Eugene . . . Eugene . . . Are you with us, Mr. McGillicudy?"

Eugene finished marking his Captain Awesome scorecard. The score was Captain Awesome 2, Pollinator 0. He closed the notebook and slid it into his desk.

"Yes, Ms. Beasley," he replied.

"It's your turn," she said.

Of course it was Eugene's turn. Isn't that always the way it works? Teachers have their own superpower. They get you right when you're thinking really important thoughts about how many times you've saved the world and crushed evil and then they ask you a question about state capitals or multiplication.

"Please come up to the board," Ms. Beasley said.

The board? Eugene swallowed hard. That was the last place any kid wanted to be: in front of the class answering a question. It was always dangerous to write on the board with all your class-mates watching your every move. Every mistake was there for the whole class to see.

I'd rather eat beets, Eugene thought.

That's when Ms. Beasley shared her plans. "I want you to spell out one of the words that will be on tomorrow's spelling test."

GULP!
SPELLING?!
TEST?!

Eugene shuffled his feet across the floor and made his way to the board. Charlie held out his hand as Eugene scuffed past.

"Good luck," Charlie whispered. "You can do it, Captain Awesome!"

Eugene gave a smile. He *really* wanted to change into his Captain Awesome superhero outfit, but he was in front of the whole class!

As Eugene continued to the board, he passed by Meredith Mooney's desk. She did *not* whisper.

She liked her insults to be loud. She also liked to dress in pink from head to toe. If you poured pink lemonade into a forty-seven-inch-tall glass and floated a pink ribbon on top, you'd get the idea about just how pink Meredith looked most days.

"Dazzle us with your brains, Poo-gene," she said. "Remember, 'Duh' starts with a *capital D*." Then she stuck out her tongue.

"Meredith!" Ms. Beasley said, silencing her. "Eugene, your word is 'boat.'"

"Boat," Eugene repeated.

He looked at the board, ready to write, but his mind went blank. It was like someone had turned the lights off in his brain. He couldn't think of letters or words. His hand was frozen at his side.

Can't ... move ... my ... arm! Eugene realized. *What kind of villain could be doing this?!*

He looked all around the room. Could it

be Meredith (aka Little Miss Stinky Pinky)? No. She was busy drawing pink unicorns in her notebook and even *she* couldn't draw unicorns *and* send a mind blast at the same time. And then Eugene saw her.

Alpha Betty!

The queen from Planet A-2-Z, evil Alpha Betty was determined to destroy all the letters of the alphabet and replace them with pictures of her evil kitty, Alpha Cat.

"She's the purrrrfect pet," Alpha Betty purred. "And instead of singing 'A-B-C-D-E-F-G . . .' everyone will be singing 'Alpha Cat, Alpha Cat, Alpha Cat, Alpha Cat, Alpha Cat, Alpha Cat, Alpha Cat . . .'"

"You'll not destroy any letters today!" Captain Awesome replied.

CHAPTER 3

First Prize? A Hamster Sidekick!

BY
Eugene

"**B**oat." Eugene said the word again. And then once more to be sure. "Boat."

"Yes, Eugene," Ms. Beasley said. "Boat."

In *Super Dude's Springtime Annual* No. 4, Super Dude used his superboat with superstrong spray action to defeat the Water Weasel, "the world's angriest sea mammal." Thanks to Super Dude, Salty Sue and her crusty Uncle Crusty had been saved.

Eugene knew how to spell "water," but "boat" might be diffi-cult. *I know it starts with* b, Eugene thought. *And it has to end with a* t.

And somewhere along the way there had to be an o. A *long* o. And an *a* in the middle. But in what order? Which! One! Came! First!

Eugene ran the question through his superpowered brain.

Eugene figured that since *a* is the first letter of the alphabet, it must be first. That made *o* the letter after it. He carefully wrote *b-a-o-t* under the chalk drawing of a boat on the board.

MISSION. ACCOMPLISHED.

Eugene put the chalk down

in the tray and looked at the word again. It looked funny. Not funny like a funny joke, but funny like something was wrong with it.

And then he realized the horrible truth.

He'd spelled the word wrong.

Oh, why couldn't his word have been "captain" or "awesome"— words he could spell in his sleep? How could he get "boat" so very wrong? It only had four letters!

Eugene's heart sank into a vat of bubbling hot lava and dropped to the bottom. Or at least that's what it felt like. His stomach rumbled. He knew what was next: Meredith.

"*B-A-O-T?!* What's a ba-ot?!" Meredith exclaimed. She laughed, and several of her friends joined in as Meredith sang, "Row, row, row your ba-ot gently

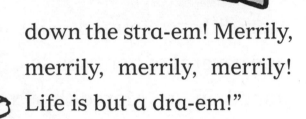

down the stra-em! Merrily, merrily, merrily, merrily! Life is but a dra-em!"

Charlie wanted to change into Nacho Cheese Man and help his best friend rearrange the letters in "baot" with the help of a can of his spray cheese.

But now it was too late to fix anything.

Fortunately, Ms. Beasley, a teacher who was on the side of goodness, quieted the class. The laughter stopped. Eugene quickly erased his misspelled word and ran back to his desk.

"Okay, listen up," Ms. Beasley said. "Everyone needs to study their words tonight. Tomorrow's our weekly spelling test."

GULP.

"And I have some exciting news, class," Ms. Beasley said.

Eugene leaned forward in his seat. He didn't want to miss a single word.

"Whoever has the highest grade on tomorrow's spelling test gets a special prize," said Ms. Beasley.

Eugene loved prizes. Would it be a trip to the Sunnyview Memorial Zoo to see the elephants—Eugene's

favorite? Or a treasure chest of pirate gold? Or maybe, just maybe, pizza for lunch for a whole week?

Nope.

It wasn't any of those things. It was something better . . . and fuzzier.

"That student gets extra Turbo Time during Turbo Day tomorrow afternoon!"

EXTRA TURBO TIME!

The class erupted in cheers.
The only thing better than Turbo
Time was *extra* Turbo Time! Eugene
thought this was better than extra
TV time or extra video game time!

Turbo was the class hamster,
but the fuzzy little fur ball had a
secret. He was also a member of the
Sunnyview Superhero Squad and

Captain Awesome's sidekick in the nonstop battle of crushing evil.

And in that battle of good vs. evil, who doesn't need the power of a superhamster?

Eugene was going to win extra Turbo Time, and no letter of the alphabet was going to stop Eugene from doing that!

CHAPTER 4

Super Tree House Study Sesh

By
Eugene

"Emergency!" Charlie called.

"*E-m-e-r-g-e-n-c-y*," spelled out Eugene. "Emergency."

"Correct!" Charlie said.

SLAP!

They high-fived.

One word down.

Twenty-four to go!

After school the boys had assembled in the Sunnyview Superhero Squad's top secret superhero base for an emergency meeting.

"By the super MI-TEE power of Captain Awesome and the canned cheese power of Nacho Cheese Man, I call this super-emergency meeting of the Sunnyview Superhero Squad to order."

Eugene took out the ceremonial Wooden Spoon of Awesomeness and banged it on the Shoebox of Justice. **WHACK!**

Today there were three items on the Squad's agenda:

1. Spelling
2. More spelling
3. Brownies

Luckily for Charlie, there was no rule that they had to be done in that order, so he stuffed a brownie into his mouth.

Spelling was important enough to list twice, but the yumminess of Mrs. McGillicudy's homemade brownies was important too. After all, superheroes have to keep up their strength with delicious snacks.

"Melling mouldn't me a mombrem!" Charlie said, his mouth full of brownie. He swallowed and tried again.

"Spelling shouldn't be a problem. We just have to keep an eye out in case Alpha Betty returns."

But Eugene knew better than to only worry about Alpha Betty. Even though spelling was one of Captain Awesome's awesome superpowers, there was always a threat to the alphabet: Little Miss Stinky Pinky.

Just like the A-B-C-Demon used his letters of destruction against Super Dude in Super Dude No. 21, Stinky Pinky would try her best to ruin tomorrow's spelling test and take the hamster prize.

The other kids didn't know

408

Meredith was really the bad guy Little Miss Stinky Pinky. With her pink hair ribbons, pink dress, pink socks, and pink shoes, people knew her only as the pinkest girl in all of Sunnyview. Yuck.

But to Captain Awesome and Nacho Cheese Man, Meredith was really the pinkest *villain* of all. It would be just like her to ruin the spelling test so she could hamster-nap Turbo and force him to reveal the real identities of Captain Awesome and Nacho Cheese Man.

"We've got to be ready for Little Miss Stinky Pinky too," Eugene said. "She'll try to use her brain-melting powers to melt our brains during the spelling test."

Neither one of them had forgotten that Miss Stinky Pinky had once tried to steal Turbo and smuggle him out of school in her backpack.

"She's not going to get him," Eugene vowed in his most awesome superhero voice. "I will win that extra Turbo Time."

"The only way to do that is to get the high score on Ms. Beasley's spelling test tomorrow," Charlie said.

Eugene nodded. "Score," he said. "S-c-o . . ." he stopped. *Wait, what was that next letter?*

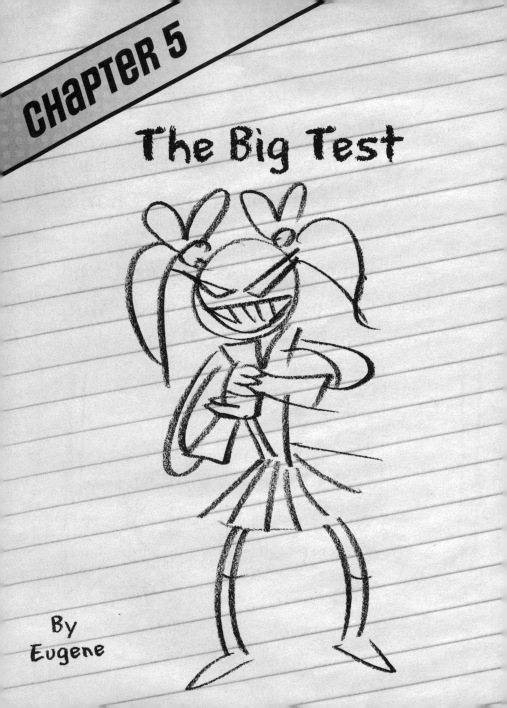

"**A**re you ready to fail, Flunk-gene?" Meredith stood in the doorway of Ms. Beasley's classroom, filling it with her rosy awfulness.

"I'm ready to *pass* my spelling test, *My! Me! Mine! MEREDITH!*" Eugene declared. "*P-A-S-S!*"

Eugene squeezed past Meredith and plopped into his desk next to Charlie.

"You ready, Charlie?" Eugene asked.

"You bet. I brought extra cans of cheese, including the new flavor: Triple Cheddar Chili! If Little Miss Stinky Pinky tries any of her tricks, my cheese shall show no mercy!"

It's always good to have some-one watch your back with a can of superhero cheese, Eugene thought.

RING!

Everyone was in their seats and Ms. Beasley was ready with

the test. "Your first word is . . .
'boat.'" She laughed. "I want to see
who was paying attention yester-
day." Eugene shook his head. That
was just the kind of thing a teacher
would do.

The second word was "carrot." The third was "chocolate." Then "waterfall."

Ms. Beasley threw out her words to the class faster than Professor Zoom-Zoom ran circles around Super Dude in Super Dude No. 96: *The Speedster of Quickitude.*

Eugene barely had time to write down an answer before the

next word hit his ears like a dodge ball in gym class.

But if aliens ever invaded Sunnyview with a list of words to spell, Eugene would be ready. He took a deep breath and summoned all his superhero might. Ms. Beasley called out the next words.

"Railroad."

"Groceries."

"Kangaroo."

Eugene caught a glimpse of Meredith

from the corner of his eye. She was writing as fast as she could.

Then Ms. Beasley said the words that froze him in his chair, just like that time the Freezer Geezer wrapped Super Dude in a giant ice cream sandwich in Super Dude No. 48.

"BONUS WORD."

A shiver ran up Eugene's back. A bonus word was one that wasn't on their study sheet. It could be any word at all.

"'Awesome,'" Ms. Beasley said.

Eugene smiled his most heroic smile. He was the first to finish. He put down his pencil with a MI-TEE *SLAP!*

Take that, Pinky, he thought as Ms. Beasley collected all the papers.

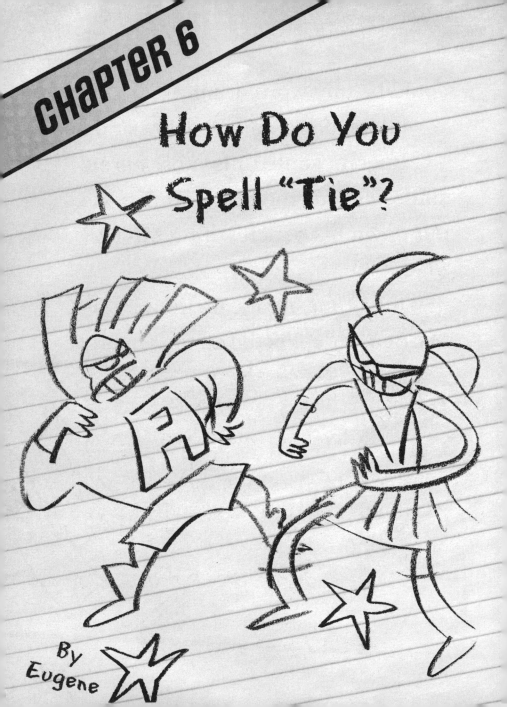

"Read quietly?" *How much longer do I have to read quietly for?* Eugene thought. It seemed to take forever plus infinity for Ms. Beasley to grade the spelling tests.

Finally she put down her red pen. "Class, I'm very pleased to announce that we have a tie for the highest grade."

Ms. Beasley pointed right at

Eugene and Meredith. "You two are tied for best speller! You'll both get extra Turbo Time today!"

GAK! thought Eugene. *Well, at least I can protect Turbo from Little Miss Stinky Pinky's evil plans!*

Mrs. Beasley continued, "I'm also excited to share that the second grade is going to have a spelling bee!"

DOUBLE GAK!

They must be called "spelling bees" because they sting when you lose, Eugene thought nervously.

"The two best spellers from

each class are going to compete for the school's spelling trophy," Ms. Beasley explained. "And I'm very happy to say that Eugene and Meredith will be representing our class!"

Eugene gasped. *Compete? In front of the school? At least Ms. Beasley's happy about it*, he thought.

But Eugene couldn't back out. There was a trophy on the line! Everyone knew that trophies weren't just a symbol of greatness. They had special trophy powers

that must only be used for good and never for evil.

This spelling bee would be the ultimate battle—not just between Eugene and Meredith, but also between Captain Awesome and Little Miss Stinky Pinky.

There could only be one winner. And it had to be Eugene. The safety of Sunnyview Elementary—and the universe—depended on it!

"I just know you'll win," Sally Williams told Eugene.

For the rest of the week Eugene spelled wherever he went.

"*B-r-o-c-c-o-l-i*," he spelled at the dinner table where his parents were used to spelling outbursts from their son. He even spelled "rutabaga," even though he was

sure that no one ever spelled it . . .
or ate it.

"*B-e-d-r-o-o-m*," he spelled in
his room, along with "blanket," "pillow," and "door."

"*T-o-i-l-e-t*," he spelled in the bathroom. And just to be sure, he spelled "*p-o-t-t-y*," too.

He even studied with Turbo. "*H-a-m-s-t-e-r*," he spelled, and he thought he saw Turbo give him a little nod.

SUNNYVIEW ELEMENTARY SPELLING BEE

Eugene had spent the rest of the week *s-p-e-l-l-i-n-g* every word he could think of until the big day finally arrived. Eugene stood on stage in the auditorium. Unfortunately, he had to stand next to Meredith because they were from the same class.

Ms. Beasley sat in the front row with the other two spelling bee judges: the school librarian and another second grade teacher named Ms. Eckles.

Behind them sat the second-grade students who were not in the bee, and behind them sat parents and family members.

"Thank you all for coming today," Ms. Eckles announced with a smile. "I'm sure you're eager to see our little spellers give it their best shot, so let the bee begin!" she said.

The librarian looked over the top of her glasses and inspected the twelve second-graders lined up

on the stage: Jake Story, Gil Ditko, Olivia Simonson, Neal Chaykin, Howard Adams, Jane Romita, Wilma Eisner, Ellen Moore, Stan Kirby Jr., Dara Sim, Meredith Mooney, and Eugene.

They stood side by side, ready for whatever wordy words awaited to trick them with blends, short vowels, and silent *e*'s.

"When it is your turn, please step forward. I will read you a word and use it in a sentence. You will then spell the word. You will only have one chance to spell it correctly. Good luck to all of you."

And with that, The Ultimate

Spelling Bee finally began!

"Gil Ditko!" the librarian announced.

Gil stepped forward. He smiled at the librarian. She did not smile back. Spelling was very serious business. Gil adjusted his glasses.

"Your word is 'sound,'" said the librarian. "Don't make a *sound*."

Gil's lip quivered and he started to sweat. His hands nervously tapped his jeans. "Um, sound. *S-o-u-n-d*. Sound."

Gil let out a sigh and then smiled.

"Correct," said the librarian.

One by one each of the students stepped forward and was challenged by the librarian and her words of trickiness.

"Correct! Incorrect! Incorrect! Incorrect!" the librarian said. Boom! Boom! Boom! And just like that Wilma Eisner, Ellen Moore, and Neal Chaykin were out.

"Eugene McGillicudy!" the librarian called out.

GULP!

Eugene felt like his feet were made of glue and he was walking

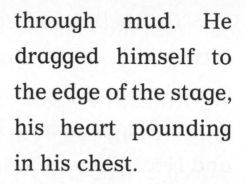

through mud. He dragged himself to the edge of the stage, his heart pounding in his chest.

I wonder if Super Dude was this nervous when he battled the Exclamation Pointer for control of Grammartopia in Super Dude No. 22, Eugene thought. He couldn't help but smile at the memory of Super Dude defeating the Pointer.

"Go, Eugene!" Charlie called

out from the audience.

"SHUSH!"cried the librarian. She raised a finger to her lips and glared at Charlie.

Oh. My. Underwear! A shocking thought suddenly hit Eugene. *Why didn't I see it before?!*

Crazy as it sounds, Eugene hadn't recognized the librarian until that moment. He had been to the library dozens of times, but today was the first time he had ever seen the librarian without a finger to her lips and saying "Shush!"

The librarian had the ability to make any student go silent with a mere glance! And if her laser stare didn't work, she'd unleash the awful fury of the Super Shush!

And now here she was, judging the spelling bee?!

Evil is full of surprises, Eugene thought.

It all made sense now. The librarian was in fact The Shusher, an evil do-badress who kept kids quiet in the library and tricked them into misspelling words!

Ms. Beasley and Ms. Eckles had no idea what evil was lurking in the chair right next to them! Eugene had to warn them! But how?!

Oh! The Sunnyview Superhero Squad Hopping Foot Code! It was his only hope! Eugene began to hop up and down on one foot.

People in the audience started to giggle.

"SHUSH!" the librarian said, sweeping her finger up to her lips. The audience instantly grew silent. Everyone knew better than to mess with The Shusher!

"Hop left twice. Small hop. Big hop. Little hop, hop, hop," Charlie said to himself as he translated Eugene's hopping code into letters. "Gfosudamuggey," Charlie read

back to himself, then smacked his forehead.

"Oh, I wish I'd paid more attention to Eugene when he explained the Sunnyview Superhero Squad Hopping Foot Code to me!" he groaned.

"Eugene? Is something wrong? Do you have to go to the bathroom?"

Ms. Beasley asked, concerned.

Eugene stopped hopping. *Next time, I'm making sure Charlie pays more attention when I explain the Sunnyview Superhero Squad Hopping Foot Code to him!* Eugene thought.

"No, Ms. Beasley," Eugene said with a sigh. "I'm ready for my word."

"Your word is 'history,'" The Shusher read from her list.

"'History,'" Eugene repeated. He closed both eyes. "Um . . . *h-i-s-t-o-r-y?*"

Eugene opened one eye in time to see Charlie burst from his chair.

"Go, Euge—"

"SHUSH!" The Shusher hissed, cutting Charlie off midcheer.

Charlie fell back into his chair. Eugene couldn't help but smile. His

superspelling powers were working perfectly.

And his hard studying didn't
hurt either.

CHAPTER 8

Evil's Favorite Word

By
Eugene

Howard Adams got nervous and added an extra *l* to the word "volume." He had to sit down.

Olivia Simonson spelled "chant" correctly and gave a happy squeal.

Then it was Meredith's turn. "Just watch and learn, Ew-gene." Meredith snarled at Eugene. She took her place at center stage. "Hello, my name is capital *M*

Meredith, capital *M* Mooney. I'd
like to thank you all for coming to
share in my victory."

"You haven't won yet, dear.

You still need to spell your words correctly," Ms. Beasley politely reminded Meredith.

"Oh, please. That's the easy part," Meredith replied.

"Meredith, your word is 'mine,'" the librarian said.

"*WHAT?* Meredith gets an easy-peasy word like 'mine?!'" Charlie whispered to Sally. "It's, like, her favorite word. Mine! Mine! Mine!"

"'Mine.' *M-i-n* . . . um, gee, what could the last letter be?" Meredith said, pretending not to know. "Oh, I don't know. Could it be . . . *e*? 'Mine.'

As in, 'The spelling bee trophy is *mine.*'" Meredith stuck her tongue out at Eugene and strolled back to her chair.

BELLS!
WHISTLES!
ALARMS!

No, not in the auditorium, but in Eugene's head. How did he not see it before?! While other students had to dodge through a maze of words with a million letters, Meredith got to spell easy words like "mine"! It could mean only one thing. . . .

The Shusher and Little Miss

Stinky Pinky were working together to make sure evil outspelled the forces of good!

Time to teach The Shusher and Little Miss Stinky Pinky a new word, Eugene thought. And that word is . . . CAPTAIN AWESOME! Eugene paused. *Wait. That's two words, isn't it?*

Eugene leaped from his chair and shouted, "MI-TEE!"

"**A**re you feeling all right, Eugene?" Ms. Beasley asked as she walked Eugene back to his chair on the stage. "You don't have to continue with the spelling bee if you don't want to. . . ."

"Oh, I want to all right," Eugene said, a big smile on his face. "I know what The Shusher and Miss Stinky Pinky are up to!"

"Ew, you are such a weirdo,

Eu-germ," Meredith whispered the moment Eugene sat down.

"A weirdo for truth, justice, and no more easy-peasy words for the bad guys during the spelling bee, you mean," Eugene replied.

The next rounds of the spelling bee went by in a blur.

"Incorrect! Correct! Incorrect! Incorrect! Incorrect!" the Shusher announced. Kids were dropping

faster than candy from a piñata. Gil Ditko, out! Jane Romita, out! Dara Sim, out! Stan Kirby Jr., out!

Soon there were only four kids left: Jake Story, Olivia Simonson, Meredith, and Eugene.

Eugene was nervous—even more nervous than the time he first tried split pea soup. It felt like the butterflies in his stomach had built a ginormous roller-coaster

and were screaming in delight as they did loop after loop after loop inside his tummy.

"Jake Story!" The Shusher said. "Your word is . . . 'browse'. As in: 'The librarian decided to browse the shelves for the right book.'"

Jake ran a hand through his red hair, which was combed back over his head. "'Browse.' B-r-o-w-z-e. 'Browse'."

"Incorrect," The Shusher said. "We love you, Jakey!" Jake's

mom called out from the audience.

The Shusher's finger was about to shoot up to her lips, but she stopped midway and lowered it slowly.

Even a bad guy understands it's pretty cool to let your son know you love him, Eugene thought.

Jake waved to his mom and dad and went back to his seat.

Olivia Simonson was next. She spelled the word "million" incorrectly.

Olivia went to sit next to Jake, leaving Meredith and Eugene.

"You might as well join them, Eu-lose," Meredith said. "There's no way you can outspell me."

"You'll never beat me!" Eugene said. "Goodness must win!"

"Ha! Yeah, right. You can't even *spell* 'victory,'" Meredith snorted.

Eugene opened his mouth, but

then stopped. *I hate it when she's right*, he thought.

"Next up, Meredith Mooney!" The Shusher announced. "Your word is . . . 'victory.' 'Victory belonged to the hero.'"

"Victory. V-i-c-t-e-r-y." Meredith

yawned. "'Victory.'" She pivoted on her foot and practically skipped back to her chair. And then she heard it.

"Incorrect!" The Shusher said.

Apparently, Meredith couldn't spell "victory" *either*.

Meredith froze. She instantly spun to face the judges. "No, I can't be wrong. Check again!"

"I'm sorry, Meredith, but you spelled the word incorrectly," The Shusher explained.

"Did not!"

"Did so."

Eugene couldn't help but smile. He loved it when bad guys argued with each other.

"Meredith, we can discuss this later, but please sit down for now,"

Ms. Beasley said in a calm voice.

Meredith's face turned redder than a tomato. It was a look her mom and dad knew very well and they covered their ears, but the explosive tantrum never came.

No shouts, no screams, no stomping. Meredith smoothed her dress, quietly sat down, and somehow managed to not make another sound.

Although she still looked like she was going to explode.

"Eugene, if you can spell 'victory,' you will then get one last word," Ms. Eckles explained.

"Victory . . . ," Eugene repeated. He looked at his shoes. There was no way he could spell the word, but he knew someone who could!

Eugene ran off the stage.

"Yes! I win!" Meredith said, jumping to her feet and thrusting both arms in the air.

"No, you do not win," Ms. Eckles informed Meredith. "And I'm sure Eugene has a perfectly good reason for . . . Oh my. . . ."

Ms. Eckles' words trailed off. She and The Shusher both stood in stunned silence. Eugene had not returned. Instead the world's mightiest hero, Captain Awesome, had taken the stage.

"Go, Captain Awesome!" called Charlie from the audience.

The Shusher was so shocked, she didn't even shush Charlie.

Ms. Eckles and The Shusher both turned to look at Ms. Beasley. Ms. Beasley was rubbing her forehead. "I know. I know. You warned me, she said to them.

Captain Awesome took a deep breath and mustered all his spelling powers. "Victory. V-i-c-t-o-r-y," he said without stopping once to take a breath. "'Victory.'"

"Correct!"The Shusher said.

The audience cheered! Captain Awesome's spelling powers were awesome!

"Eugene,"The Shusher began.

"Captain Awesome," Captain Awesome corrected.

"*Captain*. If you spell the next word, you win the spelling bee. Are you ready?"

Captain Awesome puffed out his chest and struck a heroic spelling pose. "Do your worst!" he announced in his most heroic voice ever.

"Your word is . . . 'shush'. As in: 'Shush that silly chitter-chatter.'"

Captain Awesome didn't say a word.

Tick. Tock. Tick. Tock. The sound of the clock filled the auditorium. Parents' arms grew tired of holding out their smartphones.

Time stretched like warm taffy, but Captain Awesome would not utter a sound.

"Did you hear me, young man?" The Shusher asked, breaking the silence. "I said, 'shush.'"

"But I didn't say anything," Captain Awesome replied.

"I know," The Shusher said. "And you need to spell your word or Meredith will get a chance to spell it and win the bee."

"Okay! I'm ready! Tell me my word!" Captain Awesome announced in his very most ready-to-spell voice.

"Your word is . . . 'shush.'"

"Come on!" Captain Awesome threw his hands up. "How can I spell my word if I can't speak?"

"Why can't you speak?" The Shusher asked.

"Because you keep telling me to shush!" Captain Awesome explained.

"No, Captain, that's your *word*,"
The Shusher explained.

"What's my word?"

"'Shush!'"

"But I'm not saying anything!"

Ms. Beasley interrupted them.
"Eugene, I mean, Captain, the word
you're supposed to spell *is* 'shush.'
She's not telling you *to* shush, she's
asking you to *spell* it."

"Well, why didn't you say
so!" Captain Awesome said.

The Shusher
made a face that
Captain Awesome

thought only his mom could make.

"Shush," Captain Awesome began slowly. "*S-u-s* . . ." He paused. Something was wrong. Something was missing.

And then he remembered what Super Dude always said: "Be brave. Be strong. Help others and always do your best. If you can do those things, then you'll never truly lose."

The butterflies stopped fluttering. Captain Awesome started over. "Shush . . . S-H-U-S-H. 'Shush.'"

The Shusher didn't respond. Her finger gently tapped the list of spelling words. Finally she cracked a smile. "Nice job, Captain. You win the spelling bee!"

The crowd cheered! Charlie rushed onto the stage! Ms. Beasley,

Ms. Eckles, and even The Shusher clapped!

Meredith Mooney sat in her chair, arms crossed. Her face had long ago gone past tomato and was on its way to fire-truck red.

Captain Awesome had kept the spelling bee trophy from the hands of evil! There was only one word to describe this moment . . .

MI-TEE!

479

Charlie gave Eugene a high five. "That was the most awesome thing I've seen since Super Dude defeated the Warty Wicked Witch from Wonton!" Charlie cheered. "Even Queen Stinkypants was clapping for you."

Queen Stinkypants (aka Molly McGillicudy) was Eugene's little sister.

"Thanks," Eugene said proudly.

"And check out the awesome tro-phy I got!" But as he turned to grab the trophy, he was met with . . .

SHOCK!
SURPRISE!
DOUBLE SHOCK!

The trophy was gone!

He had only turned his back on the trophy long enough to high-five Charlie and it was gone?!

"Grab your cheese, Nacho Cheese Man," Captain Awesome whispered as he scanned the auditorium. "Something stinks in this auditorium, and it's not Queen Stinkypants!"

Nacho Cheese Man quickly put on his disguise and then reached into his backpack. He pulled out a fresh can of classic nacho cheese flavor. "Let's do this," he said.

"Captain Awesome! Nacho Cheese Man!" a girl's voice cried out from behind them.

It was another superhero! And she had Meredith and the spelling bee trophy! WAIT! There was another superhero in Sunnyview?! Captain Awesome and Nacho Cheese Man were speechless.

"Hello, my name is—" Captain Awesome began, but the mysterious hero cut him off.

"I know who you are, Captain Awesome. And you, too, Nacho Cheese Man. How could I not know the two greatest superheroes in Sunnyview? Besides me, of course."

The mystery hero handed the

spelling bee trophy to Captain Awesome. "I caught Little Miss Stinky Pinky trying to sneak out the side door with your trophy."

"I wasn't really taking it! I was just borrowing it! I promise! Please don't tell anyone!" Meredith pleaded.

"Captain Awesome, it's your call. . . ," the mystery hero said.

What would Super Dude do? Captain Awesome wondered. He knew the answer.

"You're free to go, Stinky Pinky," Captain Awesome began, "but you must promise to be good and—"

"Yeah, fine, be good, whatever, I promise," Meredith said as she ran to join her parents outside.

Captain Awesome sighed, then turned to the mystery hero and said, "Thank you . . ."

But she was gone.

Captain Awesome and Nacho
Cheese Man ran outside the auditorium where the other students
enjoyed snacks with their parents.

"Who do you think it was?"
Nacho Cheese Man asked.

"Well, I know who it
wasn't," Captain Awesome
said as Meredith stuck her
tongue out at him.

The two heroes had a new mystery to solve. But it would have to
wait. Right now Captain Awesome
had a reason to celebrate. He had
won the spelling bee!

Captain Awesome and Nacho Cheese Man made their way to where their parents were waiting for them . . . and holding the biggest batch of brownies the superheroes had ever seen.

MI-TEE!

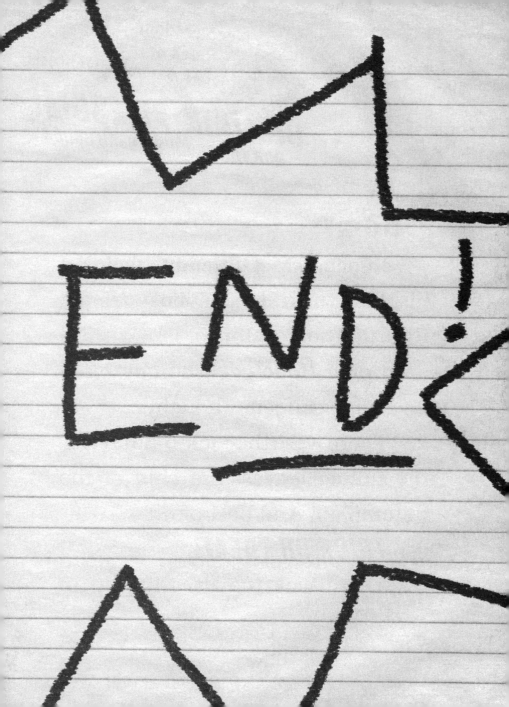

Keep reading for a sneak peek at the next Captain Awesome adventure!

CAPTAIN AWESOME
aND THE SPOOKY, SCaRY HOUSE

"**BOO!**"

Eugene McGillicudy pedaled his bike next to his best friend, Charlie Thomas Jones.

Could Halloween be any more awesome? Eugene thought.

There were the jack-o'-lanterns, the falling leaves, the chill of the autumn air. And best of all . . .

TRICK OR TREAT!

There was the dressing up in

costumes and running from house to house to collect as much candy and chocolate as your hands—or backs—could carry!

You didn't get that amount of awesomeness on Presidents' Day or even on a snow day.

And Halloween was getting closer.

Eugene and Charlie took the long way home from school. They pedaled slowly, their eyes darting from side to side. The dry fall leaves swirled across the street and crunched under the wheels of their bikes.

The town of Sunnyview went all out for Halloween. Houses

were covered in fake spiderwebs and pumpkins were on every porch. One yard had a mummy in a coffin, and another had Frankenstein sitting in a rocking chair. But Eugene and Charlie weren't just enjoying the spooky scenes.

They were out on patrol.

MONSTER PATROL!

MI-TEE!

Visit
CaptainAwesomeBooks.com
for completely awesome
activities, excerpts,
tips from Turbo, and
the series trailer!